I0662552

Reprint Publishing

FOR PEOPLE WHO GO FOR ORIGINALS.

www.reprintpublishing.com

PEEPS AT PEOPLE

Being Certain Papers from the Writings of ANNE WARRINGTON WITHERUP. *Collected by* JOHN KENDRICK BANGS *With Illustrations by* EDWARD PENFIELD

NEW YORK AND LONDON
HARPER & BROTHERS PUBLISHERS
1899

CONTENTS

ILLUSTRATIONS

ILLUSTRATIONS

PEEPS AT PEOPLE

NANSEN

NANSEN

—

IT was in the early part of February last that, acting under instructions from headquarters, I set forth from my office in London upon my pilgrimage to the shrines of the world's illustrious. Readers everywhere are interested in the home life of men who have made themselves factors in art, science, letters, and history, and to these people I was commissioned to go. But one restriction was placed upon me in the pursuit of the golden Notoriety, and that was that I should spare no expense whatever to attain my ends. At first this was embarrassing. Wealth suddenly acquired always is. But in time I overcame such difficulties as beset me, and soon learned to spend thousands of dollars with comparative ease.

And first of all I decided to visit Nansen. To see him at home, if by any possibility Nansen could be at home anywhere, would enable me to open my series interestingly. I remembered distinctly that upon his return from the North Pole he had found my own people too cold for comfort. I called to mind that, having travelled for months seeking the Pole, he had accused my fellow-countrymen of coming to see him out of "mere curiosity," and I recalled at the same time that with remarkable originality he had declared that we heated our railway trains to an extent which suggested his future rather than his past. Wherefore I decided to visit Nansen to hear what else he might have to say, while some of the incidents of his visit were fresh in our minds.

The next thing to discover, the decision having been reached, was as to Nansen's whereabouts. Nobody in London

seemed to know exactly where he might
be found. I asked the manager of the
house in which I dwelt, and he hadn't
an idea—he never had, for that matter.
Then I asked a policeman, and he said he
thought he was dancing at the Empire,
but he wasn't sure. Next I sought his
publishers and asked for his banker's
address. The reply included every bank
in London, with several trust companies
in France and Spain. To my regret, I
learned that we Americans hold none of
his surplus.

"But where do you send his letters?"
I demanded of his publisher, in despair.

"Dr. Nansen has authorized us to destroy them unopened," was the reply.
"They contain nothing but requests for
his autograph."

"But your letters to him containing
his royalties—where do they go?" I demanded.

"We address them to him in our own
care," was the answer.

"And then?" I queried.

"According to his instructions, they are destroyed unopened," said the publisher, twisting his thumbs meditatively.

It seemed hopeless.

Suddenly an idea flashed across my mind. I will go, I thought, to the coldest railway station in London and ask for a ticket for Nansen. A man so fastidious as he is in the matter of temperature, I reasoned, cannot have left London at any one of their moderately warm stations. Where the temperature is most frigid, there Nansen must have gone when leaving, he is such a stickler for temperature. Wherefore I went to the Waterloo Station —it is the coldest railway station I know —and I asked the agent for a ticket for Nansen.

He seemed nonplussed for a moment, and, to cover his embarrassment, asked:

"Second or third class?"

"First," said I, putting down a five-pound note.

"Certainly," said he, handing me a ticket to Southampton. "Do you think

6

"I BOARDED A PJINE RJAFT"

you people in the States will really have war with Spain ?"

I will not dilate upon this incident. Suffice it to say that the ticket man sent me to Southampton, where, he said, I'd be most likely to find a boat that would carry me to Nansen. And he was right. I reached Sjwjcktcwjch within twenty-four hours, and holding, as I did, letters of introduction from President McKinley and her Majesty Queen Victoria, from Richard Croker and Major Pond, Mr. Nansen consented to receive me.

He lived in an Esquimau hut on an ice - floe which was passing the winter in the far - famed Maelstrom. How I reached it Heaven only knows. I frankly confess that I do not. I only know that under the guidance of Svenskjold Bjon-stjon I boarded a plain pjine rjaft, such as the Norwegians use, and was pjaddjled out into the seething whirlpool, in the midst of which was Nansen's more or less portable cottage.

When I recovered I found myself seated

inside the cottage, which, like everything else in the Maelstrom, was waltzing about as if at a military ball or Westchester County dance.

"Well," said my host, looking at me coldly. "You are here. *Why* are you here?"

"Mr. Nansen?" said I.

"The very same," said he, taking an icicle out of his vest pocket and biting off the end of it.

"The Polar Explorer?" I added.

"There is but one Nansen," said he, brushing the rime from his eyebrows. "Why ask foolish questions? If I am Nansen, then it goes without saying that I am the Polar Explorer."

"Excuse me," I replied. "I merely wished to know." And then I took a one-dollar bill from my purse. "Here, Mr. Nansen, is my dollar. That is, I understand, the regular fee for seeing you. I should like now to converse with you. What is your price per word?"

"Have you spoken to my agents?" he asked.

8

"'MR. NANSEN ?' SAID I"

"No," said I.

"Then it will only cost you $160 a word. Had you arranged through them, I should have had to charge you $200. You see," he added, apologetically, "I have to pay them a commission of twenty per cent."

"I understand that," said I. "I have given public readings myself, and after paying the agent's commission and travelling expenses I have invariably been compelled to go back and live with my mother for six months."

"Miss Witherup," said Nansen, rising, "you did not intend to do it, and I therefore forgive you, but for the moment you have made me feel warmly towards you. Please do not do it again. Frigidity is necessary to my business. What can I do for you?"

"Talk to me," said I.

He immediately froze up again. "What about?" said he. "The Pole?"

"No," said I. "About America."

"I cannot!" he cried, despairingly.

9

"I do not wish to dwell upon my sufferings. If I told about my American experience, people would not believe; they
would rank me with Munchausen, my
sufferings were so intense. Let me tell
of how I lived on Esquimau dog-chops
and ice-cream for nineteen weeks."

"Pardon me, Mr. Nansen," said I,
"but I can't do that. We Americans
know all about the North Pole. Few of
us, on the other hand, know anything
about America, and we wish to be enlight-
ened. What did you think of Chicago?"

"Chicago? H'm! Let me see," said
Nansen, tapping his forehead gently with
an ice-pick. "Chicago! Oh yes, I remember; it was a charmingly cold city,
full of trolley-cars, and having a newly
acquired subway and a public library. I
found it a beautiful city, madam, and the
view from the Bunker Hill Statue of
Liberty was superb, looking down over
Blackwell's Island through the Golden
Gate out into the vast, trackless waste of
Lake Superior. Yes, I thought well of

it. If I remember rightly, we took in
$1869 at the door."

I was surprised at his command of details, and resolved further to test his
memory.

"And Philadelphia, Mr. Nansen?"

"A superb city, considering its re-
cency, as you say in English. I met
many delightful people there. Senator
Tom Reed received me at his palace on
Euclid Avenue, if I remember the street
aright; the Mayor of the city, Mr.
McKinley, gave me a dinner, at which I
sat down with Mr. Cleveland and Mr.
Van Wyck, and Mr. Bryan and Mr. Pulit-
zer, and other members of his cabinet;
and in my leisure hours I found the thea-
tres of Philadelphia most pleasing, with
Mr. Jefferson singing his nigger songs,
Mr. Mansfield in his inimitable skirt-
dancing, and, best of all, Mr. Daly's
Shakespearian revivals of 'Hamlet' and
'Othello,' with Miss Rehan in the title-
rôles. Oh yes, Miss Witherdown—"

"Witherup!" I snapped, coldly.

"Excuse me, Witherup," said the great explorer. "Oh yes, Miss Witherup, I found America a most delightful country, especially your capital city of Philadelphia."

"Herr Nansen," said I, "are you as accurate in your observations of the North Pole as in your notes of the States, as expressed to me?"

"Neither more nor less so," said he, somewhat uneasily, I thought.

"But you have drawn a most delightful picture of the States," said I. "I think all Americans will be pleased by your reference to the Bunker Hill Monument at Chicago, and Mayor McKinley's cabinet at Philadelphia. On the other hand, you spoke of intense suffering while with us."

"Yes," said he, "I did—because I suffered. Have you ever travelled in your own country, madam?"

"I am an American," said I. "Therefore when I travel I travel abroad."

"Then you do not know of the pri-

"DINED WITH THE CABINET"

vations of American travel," he cried. "Consider me, Nansen, compelled, after the delightful discomfort of the *Fram*, to have to endure the horrid excellence of your Pullman service. Consider me, Nansen, after having subsisted on dogs and kerosene oil for months, having to eat a breakfast costing a dollar at one of your American hotels, consisting of porridge, broiled chicken, deviled kidney, four kinds of potatoes, eggs in every style, real coffee, and buckwheat cakes! Consider me—"

"Nansen?" I inquired.

"Yes, Nansen," said he. "Consider me, Nansen, used to the cold of the Arctic regions, the Arctic perils, having to wake up every morning in an American hotel or an American parlor-car, warm, without peril, comfortable, *without anything whatsoever to growl about.*"

"It must have been devilish," said I.

"It was," said he.

"Well, Mr. Nansen," I put in, rising, "you can stand it. You are cold enough to stay in Hades for forty-seven years without losing your outside garments. How much do I owe you?"

"Fifteen thousand dollars, please," said he.

I gave him the money and swam away.

"Good-bye," he cried, as I reached the outer edge of the Maelstrom. "I hope, next time I go to America, that I shall meet you."

"Many thanks," said I. "When do you expect to come?"

"Never," he replied, "Deo volente!"

Charming chap, that Nansen. So warm, you know.

MR. HALL CAINE

MR. HALL CAINE

I DO not know why it should have happened so, but it did happen that after my interview with Nansen I felt gloomy in my soul, and hence naturally sought congenial company. My first inclination was to run down to Greece and take luncheon with King George, but when I came to look over my languages, the only bit of Greek I could speak fluently turned out to be hoi polloi, and from private advices I gather that that is the only bit of Greek that his honor the King has no use for. Therefore I bought a ticket straight through to Gloomster Abbey, Isle of Man—the residence of Hall Caine.

Appropriately enough, it was midnight

when I arrived. It was a moonlight night, but there were a dozen clouds on the horizon and directly in the wake of the moon's rays, so that all was dark. From the abbey itself no single ray of light gleamed, and all was still, save the croaking of the tree-toads in the moat, and the crickets on the roof of the parapet.

Any one else would have been chilled to the marrow; but I, having visited Nansen, had to use a fan to overcome the extreme cordiality of the scene. With the thermometer at 32° I nearly swooned with the heat.

"Is this Gloomster Abbey?" I asked of my hackman.

"Yes," said he; "and, for Humanity's sake, pay your fare and let me go. I am the father of seven orphans, and the husband of their widowed mother. If I stay here ten minutes I'll die, and my wife will marry again, Heaven help her!"

I paid him £6 10s. 6d. and let him go. He was nothing to me, but his family had my sympathy.

18

"'IS THIS GLOOMSTER ABBEY?' I ASKED"

Then I knocked on the portcullis with all my might, and was gratified to find that, like a well - regulated portcullis, it fell, and with a loud noise withal.

An intense silence intervened, and then out of the blackness of the blue above me there came a voice with a reddish tinge to it.

"Who's there?" said tho voice. "If you are a burglar, come in and rob. If you are a friend, wait a minute. If you are an interviewer from an American Sunday newspaper, accept my apologies for keeping you waiting, turn the knob, and walk in. I'll be down as soon as I can get there."

It was Hall Caine himself who spoke.

I turned the knob and walked in. All was still, dark, and cold, but I did not mind, for it fitted into my mood exactly.

In the darkness of the corridor within I barked what if I were a man I should call my shins. As it happened, being a woman, I merely bruised my ankles, when he appeared—Hall Caine himself. There

19

was no gas-light, no electric light. Nothing but the blackness of the night, and *He Appeared!* I suppose it was all due to the fact that he is a brilliant man, who would shine anywhere. However it may have been, I suddenly became conscious of a being that walked towards me as plainly discernible as an ocean steamship at sea at night, with every electric light burning in the saloon, and the red and green lanterns on the starboard and port sides of its bow.

"Mr. Caine?" said I, addressing his starboard side.

"That's I," said he, grammatically and with dignity. A man less great would have said "That's me," which is why in the darkness I knew it was Mr. Caine and not his hired man I was speaking to —or with, as your style may require.

"Mr. Caine," said I, not without nervousness, "I have come—"

"So I perceive," said he ; and then an inspiration came to me.

"—to lay my gloom at your feet," I

20

HE APPEARED !

said, with apparent meekness. "It is all I have, but such as it is you are welcome to it. Some people would have brought you rich gifts in gold and silver; some would have come with compliments and requests for your autograph; I bring you only a morbid heart bursting with gloom. Will you take it?"

"I appreciate the courtesy, madame," replied the great man, wiping a tear from the end of his nose, which twinkled like a silver star in the blackness of the corridor, "but I cannot accept your offering. I have more gloom on hand than I know what to do with. I am, however, deeply touched, and beg to offer you the hospitality of the moat, unless you have further business with me at my regular rates."

A dreadful, blood-curdling wail, like that of a soul in torment, interrupted my answer. It seemed to come from the very centre of the earth directly beneath my feet. I was frozen with horror, and my host, with a muttered imprecation, turned and ran off.

"I haven't time to see you now," he cried, as he disappeared down the steps of a yawning hole at the far end of the corridor. "I can't afford to miss the experiment for anything so small and cheap as a morbid heart bursting with gloom."

I followed closely after, although he had not granted permission. I didn't feel that I could afford to miss the experiment either, and ere he had time to slam to the door of the dungeon which we ultimately reached, I was inside his workshop.

If it was chill without, it was deadly within, save that the darkness was not so intense, red lights burning dimly in each of the four corners of the dungeon. The walls were covered with a green trickling ooze from the moat, and under foot the ground was dank and almost mushy.

In the very centre of the place was a huge rack, a relic of some by-gone age of torture, and stretched at full length upon it was a man of, I should say, about forty years of age. Two flunkies in livery— red plush trousers and powdered wigs—

IN THE WORKSHOP

now and then turned the screw, and with each turn horrid shrieks would come from the victim, mingled with alternate prayers and curses.

"What on earth is the meaning of this?" I cried, in horror.

"It means, madame," replied the famous author, calmly, "that I never fake. All my situations, all my passages descriptive of human emotions and sufferings, are drawn from life, and not from the imagination."

"You work from living models?" I gasped. "Why would not a lay figure do as well for torture?"

"Because lay-figures do not shriek and pray and curse. I am surprised that you should be so dull. James, turn the thumb-screw three times; and, Grimmins, take your cricket-bat and give the patient a bastinado on his right foot."

"It is a pitiless shame!" I cried.

"It is in the interest of art, madame," said the novelist, shrugging his shoulders. "Just as our surgeons have to vivisect for the advancement of science, so must I conduct experiments here in the interest of letters. My new novel has a stirring episode in it based upon the capture and torture of a newspaper correspondent in Thibet. I might, I suppose, have imagined the whole thing, but this so far surpasses the imagination that I am convinced it is the better way of getting my color."

"There isn't any doubt about that," said I; "but consider this man here, whose limbs you are stretching beyond all endurance—"

"He should regard it as a splendid sacrifice," vouchsafed the novelist, lighting a cigarette and winking pleasantly at his victim.

"Is his a voluntary sacrifice?" I demanded.

"Rather good joke that, eh, Rogers?" laughed Mr. Caine, addressing the sufferer. "This simple-minded little American girl asks if you are there because you like it. Ha! ha! What a droll idea!

24

Thinks you do this for pleasure, Rogers. Has an idea you tied yourself on there and racked yourself at first, so she has. Thinks you shriek so as to smother your laughter, which would be very inappropriate to the occasion."

The sufferer groaned deeply, and the novelist, turning to me, observed :

"No, madame. My poor unhappy friend Rogers is here against his will, I regret to say. It would be far pleasanter for me when I hear him bastinadoed to know that he derived a certain amount of personal satisfaction from it in spite of the pain, but it must be otherwise. Furthermore, in the story the newspaper man who is tortured is not supposed to like it, so that accuracy requires that I should have a man, like Rogers, who dislikes it intensely."

"And do you mean to say, sir, that you deliberately went out into the street and seized hold of this poor fellow, carried him in here, and subjected him to all this ? Why, it's a crime !"

"Not at all," replied Mr. Caine, nonchalantly. "I am no common kidnapper. I do not belong to a literary press-gang. I have simply exercised my rights as the owner of this castle. This man came here on his own responsibility, just as you have come. I never asked him any more than I asked you, and he has had to take the consequences, just as you will have to abide by whatever may result from your temerity. Rogers is a newspaper man, and he tried to get a free interview out of me by deceit, knowing that I no longer do a gratis business. It so happened that I was at that moment in need of just such a person for my experiment. I gave him the interview, and now he is paying for it."

The novelist paused, and after eying me somewhat closely for a moment, turned to his notes, lying on his desk alongside the rack, while a tremor of fear passed over me.

"Curious coincidence," he remarked, looking up from an abstract of his story.

"In my very next chapter I take up the sufferings in captivity of a young and beautiful American girl who is languishing and starving in a loathsome cell, full of reptiles and poisonous beasts, like Gila monsters and centipedes. She is to be just your height and coloring and age."

I grew rigid with horror.

"You wouldn't—" I began.

"Oh yes, I would," replied the author, pleasantly. "Would you like to see the cell?"

"I would like to see the outside of your castle!" I cried, turning to the stairs.

The novelist laughed hollowly at the expression of hopelessness that came over my face as I observed that a huge iron grating had slid down from above and cut off my retreat.

"I am sorry, Miss Witherup, but I haven't got the outside of my castle in here. If I had I'd show it to you at once," he said.

"I beg of you, sir," I cried, going down

on my knees before him. "Do let me go.
I—"

"Don't be emotional, my dear," he replied, in a nice, fatherly way. "You will
have an alternative. When I have re-
ceipted this," he added, writing out a bill
and tossing it to me—"when I have re-
ceipted this, you can go."

I glanced at the paper. It called for
£1500 for an interview of an hour and a
half, at £1000 an hour.

"If you will give me your check for
that amount, you may go. Otherwise I am
afraid I shall have to use you for a model."

"I have only £1200 in the bank," I replied, bursting into tears.

"It will suffice," said he. "Your terror
will be worth £300 to me in a short story
I am writing for the Manx *Sunday
Whirald.*"

Whereupon I wrote him a check for
£1200 and made my escape.

"I'll expose you to the world!" I roared
back at him in my wrath as I walked down
the path to the road.

"Do," he cried. "I never object to a free advertisement. By-bye."

With that I left him, and hastened back to London to stop payment on the check; but in some fashion he got the better of me, for it happened to be on a bank holiday that I arrived, and ere I could give notice to the cashier to refuse to honor my draft it had been cashed.

EMPEROR WILLIAM

EMPEROR WILLIAM

AFTER recovering from the attack of
nervous prostration which was the natural
result of my short visit to Gloomster Abbey, acting on my physician's advice I left
England for a time. Finding myself, some
weeks later, in Berlin, I resolved to call
upon his Imperial Highness William the
Second, better known as the Yellow Kid
of Potsdam.

I experienced some difficulty at first in
reaching the Emperor. Royalty is so
hedged about by etiquette that it seemed
almost impossible that I should get an audience with him at all. He was most charming about the matter, but, as he said in his
note to me, he could not forget the differ-

ence in our respective stations in life.
For an Emperor to consent to receive a
plain American newspaper woman was out
of the question. He could be interviewed
incog., however, as Mr. William Hohenzollern, if that would suit my wishes.

I replied instantly that it was not Mr.
William Hohenzollern that I wished to interview, but the German Emperor, and
unless I could see him as Emperor I did
not wish to see him at all. I added that
I might come *incog.* myself if all that was
necessary to make the whole thing regular
was that I should appear to be on a social
level with him, and instead of calling as
Miss Witherup I could call as the Mar-
chioness of Spuyten Duyville, or, if he pre-
ferred, Princess of Haarlem Heights, to
both of which titles, I assured him, I had
as valid a claim as any other lady journalist in the world—in fact, more so, since
they were both of my own invention.

Whether it was the independence of my
action or the novelty of the situation that
brought it about I do not know, but the

return mail brought a command from the Emperor to the Princess of Haarlem Heights to attend a royal *fête* given in her honor at the Potsdam Palace the next morning at twenty minutes after eleven.

I was there on the stroke of the hour, and found his Imperial Highness sitting on a small gilt throne surrounded by mirrors, having his tintype taken. This is one of the Emperor's daily duties, and one which he has never neglected from the day of his birth. He has a complete set of these tintypes ranged about the walls of his private sanctum in the form of a frieze, and he frequently spends hours at a time seated on a step-ladder examining himself as he looked on certain days in the past.

He smiled affably as the Grand High Chamberlain announced "The Princess of Haarlem Heights," and on my entrance threw me one of his imperial gloves to shake.

"Hooh!" he cried as he did so.

"Ditto hic," I answered, with my most charming smile. "I hope I do not disturb you, my dear Emperor?"

"Not in the least," he replied. "Nothing disturbs us. We are the very centre of equanimity. We are a sort of human Gibraltar which nothing can move. It is a nice day out," he added.

"Most charming," said I. "Indeed, a nicer day out than this no one could wish for."

"We are glad you find it so, madame."

"Excuse me, sire," I said, firmly— "Princess."

"Indeed yes. We had forgotten," he replied, with a courteous wave of his hand. "It could not be otherwise. We are glad, Princess, that you find the day nice out. We ordered it so, and it is pleasant to feel that what we do for the world is appreciated. We shall not ask you why you have sought this interview," he continued. "We can quite understand, without wasting our time on frivolous questions, why any one, even a beautiful

36

EXAMINING HIMSELF

American like yourself, should wish to see us in person. Are you in Berlin for long?"

"Only until next Thursday, sire," I replied.

"What a pity!" he commented, rising from the throne and stroking his mustache before one of the mirrors. "What a tremendous pity! We should have been pleased to have had you with us longer."

"Emperor," said I, "this is no time for vain compliments, however pleasing to me they may be. Let us get down to business. Let us talk about the great problems of the day."

"As you will, Princess," he replied. "To begin with, we were born—"

"Pardon me, sire," I interrupted. "But I know all about your history."

"They study us in your schools, do they? Ah, well, they do rightly," said the Emperor, with a wink of satisfaction at himself in the glass. "They indeed do rightly to study us. When one con-

siders what we are the result of! Far
back, Princess, in the days of Thor, the
original plans for William Second were
made. This person, whom we have the
distinguished and sacred honor to be, was
contemplated in the days when chaos
ruled. Gods have dreamed of him; god-
desses have sighed for him; epochs have
shed bitter tears because he was not yet;
and finally he is here, in us — incarnate
sublimity that we are!"

The Emperor thumped his chest proudly as he spoke, until the gold on his uni-
form fairly rang.

"Are we — ah — are we appreciated in
America?" he asked.

"To the full, Emperor—to the full!" I
replied, instantly. "I do not know any
country on the face of this grand green
earth where you are quoted more often at
your full value than with us."

"And — ah," he added, with a slight
coyness of manner—"we are—ah—supposed to be at what you Americans call
par and a premium, eh?"

"Emperor," said I, "you are known to us as yourself."

"Madame — or rather Princess," he cried, ecstatically, "you could not have praised us more highly."

He touched an electric button as he spoke, and instantly a Buttons appeared.

"The iron cross!" he cried.

"Not for me—oh, sire—not for me?" said I, almost swooning with joy.

"No, Princess, not for you," said the Emperor. "For ourself. We shall give you one of the buttons off our imperial coat. It is our habit every morning at this hour to decorate our imperial self, and we have rung for the usual thing just as you Americans would ring for a Manhattan cocktail."

"What!" I cried, wondering at the man's marvellous acquaintance with the slightest details of American life. "You know the —Manhattan cocktail?"

"Princess," said the Emperor, proudly, "we know everything."

And this was the man they call Willie-boy in London !

"Emperor," said I, "about the partition of China ?"

"Well," said he, "what of the partition of China ?"

"Is it to be partitioned ?"

The Emperor's eye twinkled.

"We have not yet read the morning papers, Princess," he said. "But we judge, from what we saw in the society news of last night's *Fliegende Choynal,* that there will be a military ball at Peking shortly, and that the affair will end brilliantly with a—ah—a German."

"Good !" said I. "And you will really fight England ?"

"Why not ?" said he, with a smile at the looking-glass.

"Your grandmother ?" I queried, with a slight shake of my head, in deprecation of a family row.

"She calls us Billie !" he cried, passionately. "Grandmothers can do a great many things, Princess, but no grand-

THE IMPERIAL BAND

mother that Heaven ever sent into this world shall call us Billie with impunity."

I was silent for a moment.

"Still, Emperor," I said, at last, "England has been very good to you. She has furnished you with all the coal your ships needed to steam into Chinese waters. Surely that was the act of a grandmother. You wouldn't fight her after that?"

"We will, if she'll lend us ammunition for our guns," said the Emperor, gloomily. "If she won't do that, then of course there will be no war. But, Princess, let us talk of other things. Have you heard our latest musical composition?"

I frankly confessed that I had not, and the imperial band was called up and ordered to play the Emperor's new march. It was very moving and made me somewhat homesick; for, after all, with all due respect to William's originality, it was nothing more than a slightly Prussianized rendering of "All Coons Look Alike to Me." However, I praised the work, and added that I had heard nothing like it in Wagner, which seemed to please the Emperor very much. I have since heard that as a composer he resents Wagner, and attributes the success of the latter merely to that accident of birth which brought the composer into the world a half-century before William had his chance.

"And now, Princess," he observed, as the music ceased, "your audience is over. We are to have our portrait painted at mid-day, and the hour has come. Assure your people of our undying regard. You may kiss our little finger."

"And will not your Majesty honor me with his autograph?" I asked, holding out my book, after I had kissed his little finger.

"With pleasure," said he, taking the book and complying with my request as follows :

"Faithfully your War Lord and Master,
"ME."

Wasn't it characteristic !

" ' 'WE ARE HAVING OUR PORTRAITS PAINTED ' "

MR. ALFRED AUSTIN

MR. ALFRED AUSTIN

IT was on a beautiful March afternoon that I sought out the Poet-Laureate of England in his official sanctum in London. A splendid mantle of fog hung over the street, shutting out the otherwise all too commercial aspect of that honored by-way. It was mid-day to the stroke of the hour, and a soft mellow glare suffused the perspective in either direction, proceeding from the gas-lamps upon the street corners, which, like the fires of eternal youth, are kept constantly burning in the capital city of the Guelphs.

I approached the lair of England's first poet with a beating heart, the trip-hammer-like thudding of which against my

ribs could be heard like the pounding of
the twin screws of an Atlantic liner far
down beneath the folds of my mackintosh.
To stand in the presence of Tennyson's
successor was an ambition to wish to
gratify, but it was awesome, and not a
little difficult for the nervous system.
However, once committed to the enterprise, I was not to be baffled, and with
shaking knees and tremulous hand I
banged the brazen knocker against the
door until the hall within echoed and re-
echoed with its clangor.

Immediately a window on the top story
was opened, and the laureate himself
thrust his head out. I could dimly perceive the contour of his noble forehead
through the mist.

"Who's there, who's there, I fain would know,
　Are you some dull and dunning dog?
　Are you a friend, or eke a foe?
　I cannot see you through the fog,"

said he.

　"I am an American lady journalist," I

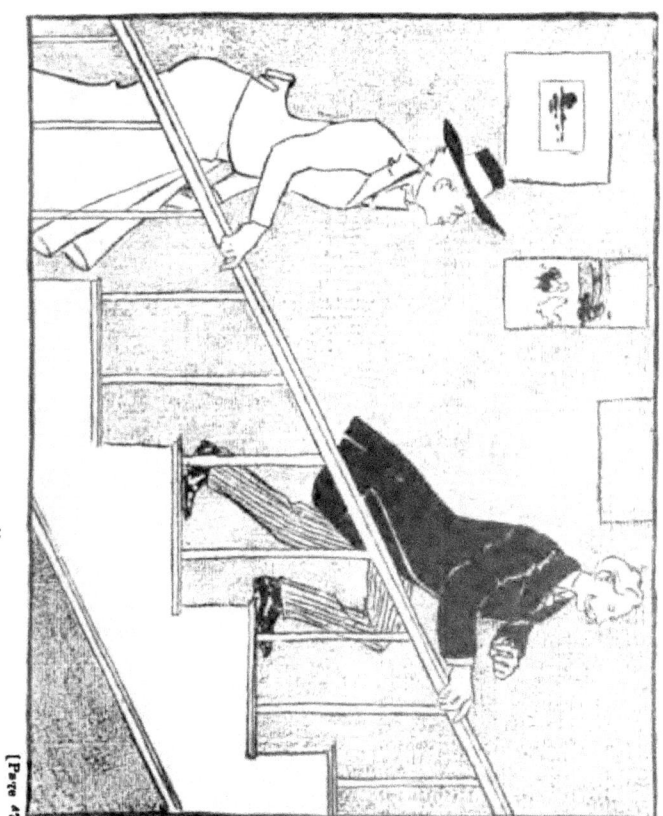

"COME RIGHT UP"

[Page 47

cried up to him, making a megaphone of my two hands so that he might not miss a word, "and I have come to offer you seven dollars a word for a glimpse of you at home."

"How much is that in £ s. d.?" he asked, eagerly.

"One pound eight," said I.

"I'll be down," he replied, instantly, and drawing his noble brow in out of the wet, he slammed the window to, and, if the squeaking sounds I heard within meant anything, slid down the banisters in order not to keep me waiting longer than was necessary. He opened the door, and in a moment we stood face to face.

"Mr. Alfred Austin?" said I.

> "The same, O Lady Journalist,
>   I'm glad to take you by the fist—
> Particularly since I've heard
>   You offer one pun eight per word."

said he, cordially grasping me by the hand. "Come right up and make yourself perfectly at home, and I'll give you an imitation of my daily routine, and will answer whatever questions you may see fit to ask. Of course you must be aware that I am averse to this sort of thing generally. The true poet cannot permit the searchlight of publicity to be turned upon his home without losing something of that delicate—"

"Hold on, Mr. Austin," said I. "I don't wish to be rude, but I am not authorized to pay you seven dollars apiece for such words as these you are uttering. If you have any explanations to offer the public for condescending to let me peep at you while at work, you must do it at your own expense."

A shade of disappointment passed over his delicate features.

"There's a hundred guineas gone at a stroke," he muttered, and for an instant I feared that I was to receive my congé. By a strong effort of the will, however, the laureate pulled himself together.

48

MR. ALFRED AUSTIN

> "If that's the case, O Yankee fair,
> Suppose we hasten up the stair,
> Where every day the Muses call,
> And waste no words here in the hall,"

said he. And then he added, courteously:
"I am sorry the elevator isn't running.
It's one of these English elevators, you
know."

"Indeed?" said I. "And what is the
peculiarity of an English elevator?"

> "Like Britons 'neath the foeman's serried guns,
> The British elevator never runs;
> For like the brain of the Scottish Thane,
> The Thane, you know, of Cawdor,
> Our lifts are always out of order,"

he explained. "It's very annoying, too,
particularly when you have to carry poems
up and down stairs."

"You should let your poems do their
own walking, Mr. Austin," said I.

"I beg your pardon," said he. "But
how can they?"

"Those I've seen have had feet enough

for a centipede," said I, as dryly as I could, considering that I was still dripping with fog.

The laureate scratched his head solemnly.

"Quite so," he said, at length. "But come, let us hasten."

We hastened upward, and five minutes later we were in the sanctum. It was a charming room. A complete set of the British Poets stood ranged in chronological sequence on the table. A copy of *Hood's Rhymster*, well thumbed, lay open on the sofa, and a volume of popular quotations lay on the floor beside the poet's easy-chair.

A full-length portrait of her Majesty the Queen, seven inches high and sixteen wide, hung over the fireplace, and beneath it stood a charming bust of the late Lord Tennyson with the face turned towards the wall.

"A beautiful workshop," said I. "Surely one sees now the sources of your inspiration."

50

" ' A BEAUTIFUL WORKSHOP,' SAID I "

"'Tis true my dear. 'Tis very, very true.
   Here in my sanctum, high above the pave,
     ma'am,
 I can't help doing all the things I do,
   Not e'en my great immortal soul to save,
     ma'am.
You see, a man who daily has to write
   Of things of which Calliope doth side-talk,
Must get above the earth and leave the
    wight
   Who dully plods along along the side-
    walk,"

he answered. "That's why I live under
the roof instead of hiring chambers on the
ground-floor. Up here I am not bothered
by what in one of my new poems I shall
call 'Mundane Things.' Rather good expression that, don't you think ? The first
draft reads :

    "'Mundane things, mundane things,
     Hansom cabs and finger rings,
     Drossy glitter and glittering dross,
     May I never come across
     Merely mundane, mundane things.'

Rather clever, to be tossed off on a

scratch pad while taking a shower-bath, eh ?"

" Yes," said I. "What suggested it ?"

"The merest accident. I got some soap in my eye and was about to give way to my temper, when I thought to myself that the true poet ought to rise above petty annoyances of that nature— in other words, above mundane things."

"Wonderfully interesting," I put in. "Was your appointment a surprise to you, Mr. Austin ?"

"Surprise ? Nay, nay, my lovely maid.
    Pray why should I surpriséd be ?
  Despite that Fortune's but a fickle jade,
    I knew the thing must come to me,
    For in these days commercial, don't you see,
      From eyes like mine no thing can e'er be
        hid ;
  And when they advertised for poetry,
    'Twas I put in the very lowest bid,"

he replied. "You see, as a newspaper man I knew what rates the other poets were getting. There was Swinburne getting seven bob a line, and Sir Edwin

Arnold asking a guinea a yard, and old Kipling grinding it out for one and six per quatrain, and Watson doing sonnets on the Yellow North, and the Red, White, and Blue East, and the Pink Sow'west, at five pounds a dozen. So when Salisbury rang me up on the 'phone and said I'd better put in a bid for the verse contract, I knew just how to arrange my rates to get tue work."

"You had a great advantage over the others," said I.

"Which shows the value of a newspaper training. Newspaper men know everything," he said. "I had but one fear, and that was your American poets. They are hustlers, and I didn't know but that some enterprising American like Russell Sage or Barnum & Bailey would form a syndicate and corner America's poem-supply, and bowl my wickets from under me. Working together, they could have done it, but they didn't know their power, thank Heaven!—if I may borrow an Americanism."

"Well, Mr. Austin," said I, rising, "I am afraid I shall have to go. I fear your words have already exceeded the appropriation. Ah—how much do I owe you?"

The laureate took from beneath his chin a small golden object that looked like a locket. Opening it, he scanned it closely for a moment.

"My chinometer says nine hundred and sixty-three words. Let us call it a thousand—I don't care for trifles," said he.

"Very well," I replied. "That is $7000 I owe you."

"Yes," he said. "But of course I allow you the usual discount."

"For what?" said I.

"Cash," said he. "Poole does it on clothes, and I've adopted the system. It pays in the end, for, as I say in my next ode to the Queen, to be written on the occasion of her Ruby Jubilee, 'A sovereign in hand is worth two heirs-presumptive in the bush.'"

54

CONSULTING HIS CHINOMETER

"In other words, cash deferred maketh the heart sick."

"Precisely. I'll put that motto down in my note-book for future use."

"I thank you for the compliment," said I, as I paid him $5950. "Good-bye, Mr. Austin."

"Good-bye, Miss Witherup," said he. "Any time when you find you have a half hour and £1000 to spare come again.

> "Say au revoir, but not good-bye,
>   For why ?
> There is no cause to whisper vale,
>   When we can parley
> Without a fear
> That words are cheap, my dear,"

said he, ushering me down-stairs and bowing me out into the fog, which by this time had lightened so that I could see the end of my nose as I walked along.

ANDREW LANG

ANDREW LANG

SEVERAL days after the exhilarating interview with the Poet-Laureate of England, I was honored by a dinner given to me by the Honorable Company of Lady Copy-Mongers at their guildhall in Piccadilly Circus, S.W. It was a delightful affair, and I met many ladies of prominence in literary fields. Miss Braddon and John Oliver Hobbes were there, and one rather stout old lady, of regal manner, who was introduced as Clara Guelph, but whom I strongly suspected to be none other than the authoress of that famous and justly popular work, *Leaves from My Diary in the Highlands, or Sixty Years a Potentate.* She was very gracious to me, and promised to send me an autograph copy of her publisher's circular.

Most interesting of all the persons encountered at the banquet, however, was Miss Philippa Phipps-Phipps, forewoman of the Andrew Lang Manuscript - Manufacturing Company, from whom I gained much startling information which I am certain will interest the public.

In the course of our conversation I observed to Miss Phipps-Phipps, of whom I had never heard before, that nothing in modern letters so amazed me as the output of Andrew Lang, for both its quality and its quantity. The lady flushed pleasurably, and said, modestly :

" We try to keep up to the standard, Miss Witherup. As a worker in literary fields, you perhaps realize how hard it is to do this, but of one thing I assure you— we have never in the last ten years allowed a bit of scamp work of any description to go out of our factory. Of course we have grades of work, but the lower grades do not go out with the Lang mark upon them."

TRADE-MARK.   NONE GENUINE WITHOUT IT

I looked at Miss Phipps-Phipps in a puzzled way, for the full import of her words did not dawn upon me instantly.

"I don't quite understand," said I. "We? Who are we?"

"The Lang Manuscript-Manufacturing Company," explained the young woman. "You are aware, of course, that Andrew Lang is not an individual, but a corporation?"

"I certainly never dreamed it," said I, with a half-smile.

"How could it be otherwise?" asked Miss Phipps-Phipps. "No human being could alone turn out an average of 647,-000,000 words a year, Miss Witherup, not even if he could run two type-writers at once, and write with his feet while dictating to a stenographer. It would be a physical impossibility."

"Dear me!" I cried in amazement. "I knew that there were thousands of articles from Lang every year, but 647,-000,000 words! Why, it is incredible!"

"That is only the average, you know,"

said Miss Phipps-Phipps, proudly. "In good years we have run as high as 716,-000,346 words; and this year, if all goes well and our operatives do not strike, we expect to turn out over 800,000,000. We have signed contracts to deliver 111,-383,000 words in the month of June alone—mostly Christmas stuff, you know, to be published next November. Last month we turned out 39,000 lines of poetry a day for twenty-five working-days, and our essay-mill has been running overtime for sixteen weeks."

"Well, I am surprised!" said I. "Yet, when I come to think of it, there is no reason why I should be. This is an age of corporations."

"Precisely," said Miss Phipps-Phipps. "Furthermore, ours had a philanthropic motive at the bottom of it all. Here was Mr. Lang simply killing himself with work, and some 700 young men and women of an aspiring turn of mind absolutely out of employment. The burdens of the one, we believed, could be made to

62

relieve the necessities of the other, and we made the proposition to Mr. Lang to make himself over to us, promising to fill his contracts and relieve him of the necessity of doing any further literary work for the rest of his life. We incorporated him on a basis of £2,000,000, giving him £1,000,000 in shares. The rest was advertised as for sale, and was oversubscribed ten to one. Workshops were built at Woking, and as a starter 600 operatives were employed. Working night and day, at the end of the first year we were just three months behind our orders. We immediately doubled our force to 1200, and so it has gone until to-day, and the business is constantly increasing. Our stock is at a premium of 117%, and we keep 3750 people, with a capacity of 10,000 words a day each, constantly employed."

"I am astonished!" I cried. "The magnitude of the work is appalling. Are your shops open to visitors?"

"Certainly. I shall be pleased if you

will come out to Woking to-morrow, and
I will show you over the establishment,"
replied Miss Phipps-Phipps, courteously.
And then for the moment the conversation stopped.

The next day I was at Woking, where
Miss Phipps-Phipps met me at the station. A ten-minutes' drive brought us
to the factory, a detailed description of
which would be impossible in the limits
at my disposal. Suffice it to say that after an hour's walk through the various de-
partments I was still not half acquainted
with the marvels of the establishment.
In the Essay and Letters to Dead Authors
Department sixty-eight girls were driving
their pens at a rate that made my head
whirl. A whole floor was given over to
the Fairy-Tale Department, and I saw
fairy-books of all the colors in the rain-
bow being turned out at a rapid rate.

"Here," said the forelady, as we reached
a large, capacious, and well-lighted writ-
ing-room, "is our latest venture. There
are 700 employees in here, and they work

from 9 A.M. to 12, have a half hour for
luncheon, and resume. At five they go
home. They have in hand the Lang
Meredith. We have purchased from Mr.
Meredith all right and title to his complete works, which we are having rewrit-
ten. These will appear at the proper
time as ' *The Lucid Meredith*, by Andrew
Lang.' The old gentleman at the desk
over there," she added, pointing to a keen-
eyed, sharp-visaged fellow, with a long
nose and nervous manner, "is Mr. Fergus
Holmes, who began life as a detective, and
became a critic. He is here on a large
salary, and has nothing to do but use his
critical insight and detective instinct to
find the thought in some of Mr. Meredith's most complicated periods. After
all, Miss Witherup, our operators are
only human, and some of them cannot
understand Meredith as well as they
might."

"I am glad to know," said I, with a
laugh, "that you pay Mr. Fergus Holmes
a large salary. A man employed to de-

tect the thought of some of Mr. Meredith's paragraphs—"

"Oh, we understand all about that,"
Miss Phipps - Phipps smiled, in return.
"We know his value, which is very great
in this particular matter."

"And does he never fail ?" I asked.

"I presume he does, but he never gives
up.   Once he asked to be allowed to con-
sult with Mr. Meredith before giving an
opinion, and we consented.   He wrote to
the author, and it turned out that Mr.
Meredith had forgotten the paragraph entirely, and couldn't tell himself what he
meant.   But he was very nice about it.
He gave us carte blanche to make it mean
anything that would fit into the rest of
the story."

We passed on into another room.

"This room," said Miss Phipps-Phipps,
"is at present devoted to the British
poets.   There have been a great many
bad poets in Britain who have become
immortal, and we are trying to make
them good.   That young man over there

IN THE MEREDITH SHOP

with red hair is rewriting Burns—the introduction we are doing in our essay-room. The young lady in blue glasses is doing Gay over again; and we have intrusted our Lang edition of Herrick to the retired clergyman whom you see sitting on that settee by the window with a slate on his lap. To show you how completely we do our work, let me tell you that in this case of Herrick all his poems were first copied off on slates by our ordinary copyists, so that the clergyman who is doing them over again has only to wet his finger to rub out what might strike some people as an immortal line."

"It's a splendid idea!" I cried. "But wouldn't a blackboard prove less expensive?"

"We never consider expense," said Miss Phipps - Phipps. "We really do not have to. You see, with a capacity of 800,000,000 words a year at the rates for Lang, for which we pay at rates for the unknown, we are left with a margin of profit which pleases our stockholders and does not arouse the cupidity of other authors."

"What a wonderful system !" said I.

"We think it so," said Miss Phipps-Phipps, placidly.

"And do you never have any troubles ?" I asked.

"Oh yes," replied my hostess. "Only last week the Grass of Parnassus and Blue Ballade employees rose up and struck for sixpence more per quatrain. We locked them out, and to - day have filled their places with equally competent employees. You can always find plenty of unemployed and unpublished poets ready to step in. Our prose hands do not give us much trouble, and our revisers never say a word."

"Have you any novelties in hand ?" I asked.

"Oh yes," said Miss Phipps - Phipps. "We are going to supersede Boswell with *Lang's Johnson*. We are preparing a *Lang Shakespeare ;* and when the copyrights on Thackeray and Dickens have

EDITING " HERRICK "

expired, we'll do them all over again. Then we are experimenting in colors for a new fairy-book; and our chromatic Bibles will be a great thing. We are also contemplating an offer to the French Academy to permit all the works of its members to be issued as ours. I really think that *Daudet* by Andrew Lang would pay. *Hugo* by Lang might prove too much for the British public, but we shall do it, because we have confidence in ourselves. We shall issue the *Philosophy of Schopenhauer* by Andrew Lang next week."

"How about our American authors?" I queried. "Are you going to rewrite any of them?"

"Who are they?" asked Miss Phipps-Phipps, with an admirable expression of ingenuousness.

"Well," said I, "myself, and—ah—Edgar Poe."

"Any poets?" said Miss Phipps-Phipps.

"Some," I answered. "Myself and—ah—Longfellow."

"I don't know," said Miss Phipps-Phipps, becoming somewhat reserved. "Send me your manuscripts. I have heard of you, of course—but—ah—who is Miss Longfellow?"

I contented myself with a reference to the scenery, and then I said: "Miss Double Phipps, I wish you would conduct me into the presence of Mr. Lang. I like him as a manly man, and I love him for the books he has put forth, which not only show his manliness, but his appreciation of everything in letters that is good."

"Well, really, Miss Witherup," said Miss Phipps - Phipps, "we don't know where he is, but we think—it is not my thought, but that of the corporation—we think you will find him playing golf at St. Andrews."

"Thank you," said I. "But, after all," I added, "it is not what the corporation thinks so much as what you as an individual think. Where do you believe I may find Mr. Lang?"

"Among the Immortals," was the answer, spoken with enthusiasm.

And believing that the lady was right, I ceased to look for Mr. Lang, for in the presence of immortals I always feel myself to be foolish.

Nevertheless, I am very glad to have seen the Lang Company at Woking, and I now understand many things that I never understood before.

ZOLA

ZOLA

To visit a series of foreign celebrities at home without including Émile Zola in the list would be very like refusing to listen to the lines of Hamlet in Bacon's immortal tragedy of that name. Furthermore, to call upon the justly famous novelist presupposes a visit to Paris, which is a delightful thing, even for a lady journalist. Hence it was that on leaving Woking, after my charming little glimpse into the home life of the Lang Manuscript-Manufacturing Company, I decided to take a run across the Channel and look up the Frenchman of the hour. The diversion had about it an air of adventure which made it pleasantly exciting. For

ten hours after my arrival at Paris I did not
dare ask where the novelist lived, for fear
that I might be arrested and sent to Devil's
Island with Captain Dreyfus, or forced to
languish for a year or two at the Château
d'If, near Marseilles, until the government
could get a chance formally to inquire
why I wished to know the abiding-place
of M. Zola. There was added to this also
some apprehension that even if I escaped
the gendarmes the people themselves might
rise up and string me to a lamp-post as a
suitable answer to so treasonable a question.

To tell the truth, I did not go about my
business with my usual nerve and aplomb.
Had I represented only myself, I should not
have hesitated to expose myself to any or
to all danger. Intrusted as I was, however, with a commission of great importance to those whom I serve at home, it
was my duty to proceed cautiously and
save my life. I therefore went at the
matter diplomatically. For fifty centimes
I induced a small flower-girl, whom I en-

SEEKING ZOLA

countered in front of the Café de la Paix, to inquire of the head waiter of that establishment where M. Zola could be met. The tragedy that ensued was terrible. What became of the child I do not know, but when, three hours later, the troops cleared the square in front of the café, the dead and wounded amounted to between two hundred and fifty and three hundred, and the china, tables, and interior decorations of the café were strewn down the Avenue de l'Opéra as far as the Rue de l'Echelle, and along the boulevard to the Madeleine. The opera-house itself was not appreciably damaged, although I am told that pieces of steak and chops and cánned pease have since been found clinging to the third-story windows of its splendid façade.

My next effort was even more cautious. I bought a plain sheet of note-paper, and addressed it anonymously to the editor of *La Patrie*, asking for the desired information. The next morning *La Patrie* announced that if I would send my name

and address to its office the communica-
tion would be answered suitably. My
caution was still great, however, and the
name and address I gave were those of a
blanchisseuse who ran a pretty little shop
on Rue Rivoli. That night the poor
woman was exiled from France, and the
block in which she transacted business
demolished by a mob of ten thousand.

I was about to give up, when chance
favored me. The next evening, while
seated in my box at the opera, the
door was suddenly opened, and a heavy
but rather handsome-eyed brunette of I
should say fifty years of age burst in
upon me.

"Mon Dieu !" she cried, as I turned.
"Save me ! Tell them I am your chap-
eron, your mother, your sister—anything
—only save me ! You will never regret
it."

She had hardly uttered these words
when a sharp rap came upon the door.
"Entrez," I cried. "Que voulez-vous,
messieurs ?" I added, with some asperity,

CONSULTING " LA PATRIE "

as five hussars entered, their swords clanking ominously.

"Your name?" said one, who appeared to be their leader.

"Anne Warrington Witherup, if you refer to me," said I, drawing myself up proudly. "If you refer to this lady," I added, "she is Mrs. Watkins Wilbur Witherup, my—ah—my step-mother. We are Americans, and I am a lady journalist."

Fortunately my remarks were made in French, and my French was of a kind which was convincing proof that I came from Westchester County.

A great change came over the intruders.

"Pardon, mademoiselle," said the leader, with an apologetic bow to myself. "We have made the grand *faux pas*. We have entered the wrong box."

"And may I know the cause of your unwarranted intrusion," I demanded, "without referring the question to the State Department at home?"

"We sought—we sought an enemy to

France, mademoiselle," said they. "We thought he entered here."

"I harbor only the friends of France," said I.

"Vive la Witherup !" cried the hussars, taking the observation as a compliment, and then chucking me under the chin and again apologizing, with a sweeping bow to my newly acquired step - mother, they withdrew.

"Well, mamma," said I, turning to the lady at my side, "perhaps you can shed some light on this mystery. Who are you ?"

"Softly, if you value your life," came the answer. "*Zola, c'est moi !*"

"Mon Doo !" said I. "Vous ? Bien, bien, bien !"

"Speak in English," he whispered. "Then I can understand."

"Oh, I only said well, well, well," I explained. "And you have adopted this disguise ?"

"Because I have resolved to live long enough to get into the Academy," he ex-

"' SAVE ME !' SHE CRIED "

plained. "I cannot tell you how grateful I am for your timely aid. If they had caught me they would have thrown me down into the midst of the claque."

"Come," said I, rising and taking him by the hand. "I have come to Paris to see you at home. It was my only purpose. I will escort you thither."

"Non, non !" he cried. "Never again. I am much more at home here, my dear lady, much more. Pray sit down. Why, when I left home by a subterranean passage, perhaps you are not aware, over a thousand members of the National Guard were singing the 'Marseillaise' on the front piazza. Three thousand were dancing that shocking dance, the cancan, in my back yard, and four regiments of volunteers were looking for something to eat in the kitchen, assisted by one hundred and fifty pétroleuses to do their cooking. All my bedroom furniture was thrown out of the second-story windows, and the manuscripts of my new novel were being cut up into souvenirs."

"Poor old mamma!" said I, taking him by the hand. "You can always find comfort in the thought that you have done a noble action."

"It was a pretty good scheme," replied Zola. "A million pounds sterling paid to your best advertising mediums couldn't have brought in a quarter the same amount of fame or notoriety; and then, you see, it places me on a par with Hugo, who was exiled. That's really what I wanted, Miss Witherup. Hugo was a poseur, however, and if he hadn't had the luck to be born before me—"

"Ah," said I, interrupting, for I have rather liked Hugo. "And where do you wish to go?"

"To America," he replied, dramatically. "To America. It is the only country in the world where realism is not artificial. You are a simple, unaffected, outspoken people, who can hate without hating, can love without marrying, can fight without fighting. I love you."

"Sir—or rather mamma!" said I, some-

what indignantly, for as a married man
Zola had no right to make a declaration
like that, even if he is a Frenchman.

"Not you as you," he hastened to say,
"but you as an American I love. Ah,
who is your best publisher, Miss Witherup?"

I shall not tell you what I told Zola,
but they may get his next book.

"M. Zola," said I, placing great emphasis on the M, "tell me, what interested
you in Dreyfus — humanity — or literature?"

"Both," he replied; "they are the
same. Literature that is not humanity
is not literature. Humanity that does
not provide literary people with oppor-
tunity is not broad humanity, but special
and selfish, and therefore is not humanity
at all."

"Did Dreyfus write to you?" I asked.

"No," said he. "Nor I to him. I
have no time to write letters."

"Then how did it all come about?" I
demanded.

"He was attracting too much attention!" cried the novelist, passionately. "He was living tragedy while I was only writing it. People said his story was greater than any I, Émile—"

"Witherup!" said I, anxiously, for it seemed to me that the people in the next box were listening.

"Merci!" said he. "Yes, I, Mrs. Watkins Wilbur Witherup, of Westchester City, U. S. A., was told that this man's story was greater and deeper in its tragic significance than any I could conceive. Wherefore I wrote to the War Department and accused it of concealing the truth from France in the mere interests of policy, of diplomacy. *I* made them tremble. *I* made the army shiver. *I* have struck a blow at the republic from which it will not soon recover. And to-day Dreyfus pales beside the significance of Zola. I believe in free institutions, but Heaven help a free institution when it clashes with a paying corporation like Émile—"

"Witherup! Do be cautious," I put in again. "Yet, sir," I added, "they have quashed your sentence, and you need not go to jail."

"No," said he, gloomily. "I need not. Why? Because jail is safer than home. That is why they did it. They dare not exile me. They hope by quashing me to be rid of me. But they will see. I will force them to imprison me yet."

"If you are so anxious to visit America, why don't you?" I suggested. "There is no duty on the kind of thing we do not wish to manufacture ourselves."

"Ah," said he; "if I was exiled, they would send me. If I go as a private citizen, well, I pay my own way."

"Oh," said I. "I see."

And then, as the opera was over, we departed. Zola saw me to my carriage, and just as I entered it he said: "Excuse me, Miss Witherup, but what paper do you write for?"

I told him.

"It is a splendid journal!" he cried.

"I take it every day, and especially enjoy its Sunday edition. In fact, it is the only American newspaper I read. Tell your editor this, and here is my photograph and my autograph, and a page of my manuscript for reproduction."

He took all these things out of his basque as he spoke.

"I will send you to-morrow," he added, "an original sketch in black and white of my house, with the receipt of my favorite dish, together with a recommendation of a nerve tonic that I use. With this will go a complete set of my works with a few press notices of the same, and the prices they bring on all book-stands. Good-bye. God bless you!" he concluded, huskily. "I shall miss my step-daughter as I would an only son. Adieu!"

We parted, and I returned, much affected, to my rooms, while he went back, I presume, to his mob-ridden home.

SIR HENRY IRVING

SIR HENRY IRVING

THE impression left upon my mind by
my curious and intensely dramatic en-
counter with Zola was of so theatric a
nature that I resolved to get back to con-
ventional ground once more through the
medium of the stage. I was keyed up to
a high pitch of nervous excitement by my
unexpected meeting with an unsuspected
step-mother, and the easiest return to my
norm of equanimity, it seemed to me,
lay through the doors of the greenroom.
Hence I sought out London's only actor,
Sir Henry Irving.

I found him a most agreeable gentleman.
He received me cordially on the stage of
his famous theatre. There was no setting

of any kind. All about us were the bare cold walls of the empty stage, and it was difficult to believe that this very same spot, the night before, had been the scene of brilliant revels.

"How do you do, Miss Witherup?" said Sir Henry, as I arrived, advancing with his peculiar stride, which reminds me of dear old Dobbin on my father's farm. "It is a great pleasure to welcome to England so fair a representative of so fine a press."

"I wished to see you, 'at home,' Sir Henry," I replied, not desiring to let him see how completely his cordiality had won me, and so affecting a coldness I was far from feeling.

"That is why I have you *here*, madam," he replied. "The stage is my home. The boards for me; the flare of the lime-lights; the pit; the sweet family circle; the auditorium in the dim distance; the foot-lights—ah, these are the inspiring influences of *my* life! The old song 'Home Is Where the Heart Is' must, in my case, be

90

revised to favor the box-office, and instead of the 'Old Oaken Bucket,' the song I sing is the song of the 'Old Trap Door.' Did you ever hear that beautiful poem, 'The Song of the Old Trap Door'?"

"No, Sir Henry, I never did," said I. "I hope to, however."

"I will do it now for you," he said; and assisting me over the foot-lights into a box, he took the centre of the stage, ordered the calcium turned upon him, and began:

"How dear to my heart are the scenes of my
    triumphs,
  In Hamlet, Othello, and Shylock as well!
Completely confounding the critics who cry
    'Humphs!'
  And casting o'er others a magical spell!
How dear to my soul are the fond recollections
  Of thunderous clappings and stampings and
    roars
As, bowing and scraping in many directions,
  I sink out of sight through the old trap
    doors!
The old trap doors, the bold trap doors,
  That creaking and squeaking sink down thro'
    the floors!"

I could not restrain my enthusiasm when he had finished.

"Bravo !" I cried, clapping my hands together until my palms ached. "More !"

"There is no more," said Sir Henry, with a gratified smile. "You see, recited before ten or twenty thousand people with the same verve that I put into 'Eugene Aram,' or 'Ten Little Nigger Boys,' so much enthusiasm is aroused that I cannot go on. The applause never stops, so of course a second verse would be a mere waste of material."

"Quite so," I observed. Then a thought came to me which I resolved to turn to my profit. "Sir Henry," I said, "I'll bet a box of cigars against a box for your performance to-night that I can guess who wrote that poem for you in one guess."

"Done !" he replied, eagerly.

"Austin," said I.

"Make Miss Witherup out a ticket for Box A for the 'Merchant of Venice' to-night," cried the famous actor to his secretary. "How the deuce did you know ?"

"Oh, that was easy," I replied, much gratified at having won my wager. "I don't believe any one else could have thought of a rhyme to triumphs like 'cry Humphs'!"

"You have wonderful insight," remarked Sir Henry. "But come, Miss Witherup, I did not mean to receive you in a box, or on a bare stage. What is your favorite style of interior decoration?"

His question puzzled me. I did not know but that possibly Sir Henry's words were a delicate method of suggesting luncheon, and then it occurred to me that this could not possibly be so at that hour, one o'clock. Actors never eat at hours which seem regular to others. I hazarded an answer, however, and all was made clear at once.

"I have a leaning towards the Empire style," said I.

Sir Henry turned immediately and roared upward into the drops: "Hi, Billie, set the third act of 'Sans Gene,' and tell my valet to get out my Bonapartes. The lady has a leaning towards the Empire. Excuse me for one moment, Miss Witherup," he added, turning to me. "If you will remain where you are until I have the room ready for you, I will join you there in five minutes."

The curtain was immediately lowered, and I sat quietly in the box, as requested, wondering greatly what was going to happen. Five minutes later the curtain rose again, and there, where all had been bare and cheerless, I saw the brilliantly lit room wherein Bonaparte as Emperor has his interview with his ex-laundress. It was cosey, comfortable, and perfect in every detail, and while I was admiring, who should appear at the rear entrance but Bonaparte himself — or, rather, Sir Henry made up as Bonaparte.

"Dear me, Sir Henry !" I cried, delightedly. "You do me too much honor."

"That were impossible," he replied, gallantly. "Still, lest you be embarrassed by such preparations to receive you, let me say that this is my invariable custom,

94

"I SAT QUIETLY IN THE BOX"

and when I know in advance of the tastes of my callers, all is ready when they arrive. Unfortunately, I have had to keep you waiting because I did not know your tastes."

"Do you mean to say that you adapt your scenery and personal make-up to the likings of the individual who calls?" I cried, amazed.

"Always," said he. "It is easy, and I think courteous. For instance, when the Archbishop of Canterbury calls upon me I have Canterbury Cathedral set here, and wear vestments, and receive him in truly ecclesiastical style. The organ is kept going, and lines of choir-boys, suitably garbed, pass constantly in and out.

"When the King of Denmark called I had the throne-room scene of 'Hamlet' set, and we talked, with his Majesty sitting on the throne, and myself, clad as the melancholy Prince, reclining on a rug before him. He expressed himself as being vastly entertained. It gave him pleasure, and was no trouble to me beyond giving orders to the stage-manager. Then when an old boyhood friend of mine who had gone wrong came to see me, hearing that he was an inebriate, as well as a thief, I received him in the character of Dubosc, in the attic scene of the 'Lyons Mail.'"

"A very interesting plan," said I, "and one which I should think would be much appreciated by all."

"True," replied Sir Henry. And then he laughed. "It never failed but once," said he. "And then it wasn't my fault. Old Beerbohm Tree came to visit me one morning, and I had the graveyard scene of 'Hamlet' set, and myself appeared as the crushed tragedian. I thought Tree had some sense of humor and could appreciate the joke, but I was mistaken. He got as mad as a hatter, and started away in a rage. If he hadn't fallen into the grave on the way out, I'd never have had a chance to explain that I didn't mean anything by it."

By this time I had clambered back to the stage again, and was about to sit down

on one of the very handsome Empire sofas
in the room, when Sir Henry gave a leap
of at least two feet in the air, and roared
with rage.

"Send the property-man here!" he
cried, trembling all over and turning white
in the face. "Send him here; bring him
in chains. If he's up-stairs, throw him
down; if he's down-stairs, put him in a
catapult and throw him up. It matters
not how he comes, as long as he comes."

I shrank back in terror. The man's
rage seemed almost ungovernable, and I
observed that he held a poker in his hand.
Up and down the room he strode, mut-
tering imprecations upon the property-
man, until I felt that if I did not wish to
see murder done I would better withdraw.

"Excuse me, Sir Henry," said I, rising,
and speaking timidly, "I think perhaps
I'd better go."

"Sit down!" he retorted, imperiously,
pointing at the sofa with the poker. I sat
down, and just then the property-man arrived.

"Want me, S'rennery?" he said.

Irving gazed at him, with a terrible frown wrinkling his forehead, for a full minute, during which it seemed to me that the whole building trembled, and I could almost hear the seats in the top gallery creak with nervousness.

"Want you?" he retorted, witheringly. "Yes, I want you—as an usher, perhaps; as a flunky to announce that a carriage waits; as a Roman citizen to say Hi-hi! but as a property-man, never!"

There was another ominous pause, and I could see that the sarcasm of the master sank deeply into the soul of the hireling.

"Wha—what 'ave I done, S'rennery?" asked the trembling property-man.

"WHAT HAVE YOU DONE?" roared Sir Henry. "Look upon that poker and see!"

The man looked, and sank sobbing to the floor.

"Heaven help me!" he moaned. "I have a sick grandfather, S'rennery," he added. "I was up with him all night."

The great man immediately became all

98

"'SEND THE PROPERTY-MAN HERE!' HE CRIED"

tenderness. Throwing the poker to one side, he sprang to where his unfortunate property-man lay, and raised him up.

"Why the devil didn't you say so?" he said, sympathetically. "I didn't know it, Henderson, my dear old boy. Never mind the poker. Let it go. I forgive you that. Here, take this £20 note, and don't come back until your grandfather is well again."

It was a beautiful scene, and so pathetic that I almost wept. The property-man rose to his feet, and putting the £20 note in his pocket, walked dejectedly away.

Sir Henry turned to me, and said, his voice husky with emotion : "Pardon me, Miss Witherup! I was provoked."

"It was a magnificent scene, Sir Henry," said I. "But what was the matter with the poker? I thought it rather a good one."

"It is," said he, sitting down on a small chair and twiddling his thumbs. "But, you see, this is an Empire scene. and that confounded thing is a Marie Antoinette poker. Why, if that had hap-

99

pened at a public performance, I should have been ruined."

"Might not Bonaparte have used a Marie Antoinette poker?" I asked, to draw him out.

"Bonaparte, Miss Witherup," he answered, "might have done anything but that. You see, by the time he became Emperor every bit of household stuff in the palace had been stolen by the French mobs. Therefore it is fair to assume that the palace was entirely refurnished when Bonaparte came. in, and as at that time there was no craze for Louis Quinze, or Louis Seize, or Louis number this, that, and the other, it is not at all probable that Napoleon would have taken the trouble to snoop around the second - hand shops for a poker of that kind. Indeed, it is more than probable that everything he had in the palace was absolutely new."

"What a wonderful mind you must have, Sir Henry, to think of these things!" I said, enthusiastically.

"Miss Witherup," said the actor-knight,

impressively, "this is an age of wonderful minds, and there are so many of them that he who wishes to rise above his fellows must be careful of every detail. Would I have been a knight to-day had it not been for my care of details? Never. It would have gone to Willie Edouin, or to my friend Tree, or to some other actor of the same grade. My principle, Miss Witherup, is not original. I look after the details, and the results take care of themselves. It is the old proverb of the pennies and the pounds all over again."

"It is wisdom," I said, oracularly. "But it must be wearing."

"Oh no," said Sir Henry, with a gesture of self-deprecation. "There are so many details that I have had to make up a staff of advisers. As a matter of fact, I am not a man. I am a combination of men. In the popular mind I embody the wisdom, the taste, the culture, the learning of many. In fact, Miss Witherup, while I am not London, London finds artistic expression in me."

"And you are coming to America again?" I asked, rising, for I felt I ought to go, I was so awed by the humble confession of my host.

"Some day," said he. "When times are better."

"Why, Sir Henry," I cried, "you who have just given £20 to your property-man can surely afford to cross—"

"I referred, madam," he interrupted, "to times in America, for I contemplate charging $5 a stall when next I visit you. You see, my next visit will be the first of a series of twenty farewell seasons which I propose to make in the States, which I love dearly. Don't forget that, please— *which I love dearly.* I want your people to know."

"I shall not, Sir Henry," said I, holding out my hand. "Good-bye."

"Say *au revoir*," he replied. "I shall surely see you at to-night's performance."

And so we parted.

On the way down the Strand, back to

" 'IT WAS ALL ARRANGED BEFOREHAND, MISS' "

my rooms, I met the property-man, who
was evidently waiting for me.

"Excuse me, miss," said he, "but you
saw ?"

"Saw what ?" said I.

"How he called me down about the
Marie Antoinette poker ?" he replied,
nervously.

"Yes," said I, "I did."

"Well, it was all arranged beforehand,
miss, so that you would be impressed by
his love for and careful attention to details. That's all," said he. "We other
fellers at the Lyceum has some pride,
miss, and we wants you to understand
that S'rennery isn't the only genius on the
programme, by good long odds. It's not
knowin' that that made her Majesty the
Queen make her mistake."

"I didn't know, Mr. Henderson, that
her Majesty had made a mistake," said I,
coldly.

"Well, she did, miss. She knighted
S'rennery as a individual, when she'd
ought to have knighted the whole bloomin'

theaytre. There's others than him as does it !" he observed, proudly. "King Somebody knighted a piece of steak. Why couldn't the Queen knight the theaytre ?"

Which struck me as an idea of some force, although I am a great admirer of a man who, like Sir Henry, can dominate an institution of such manifest excellence.

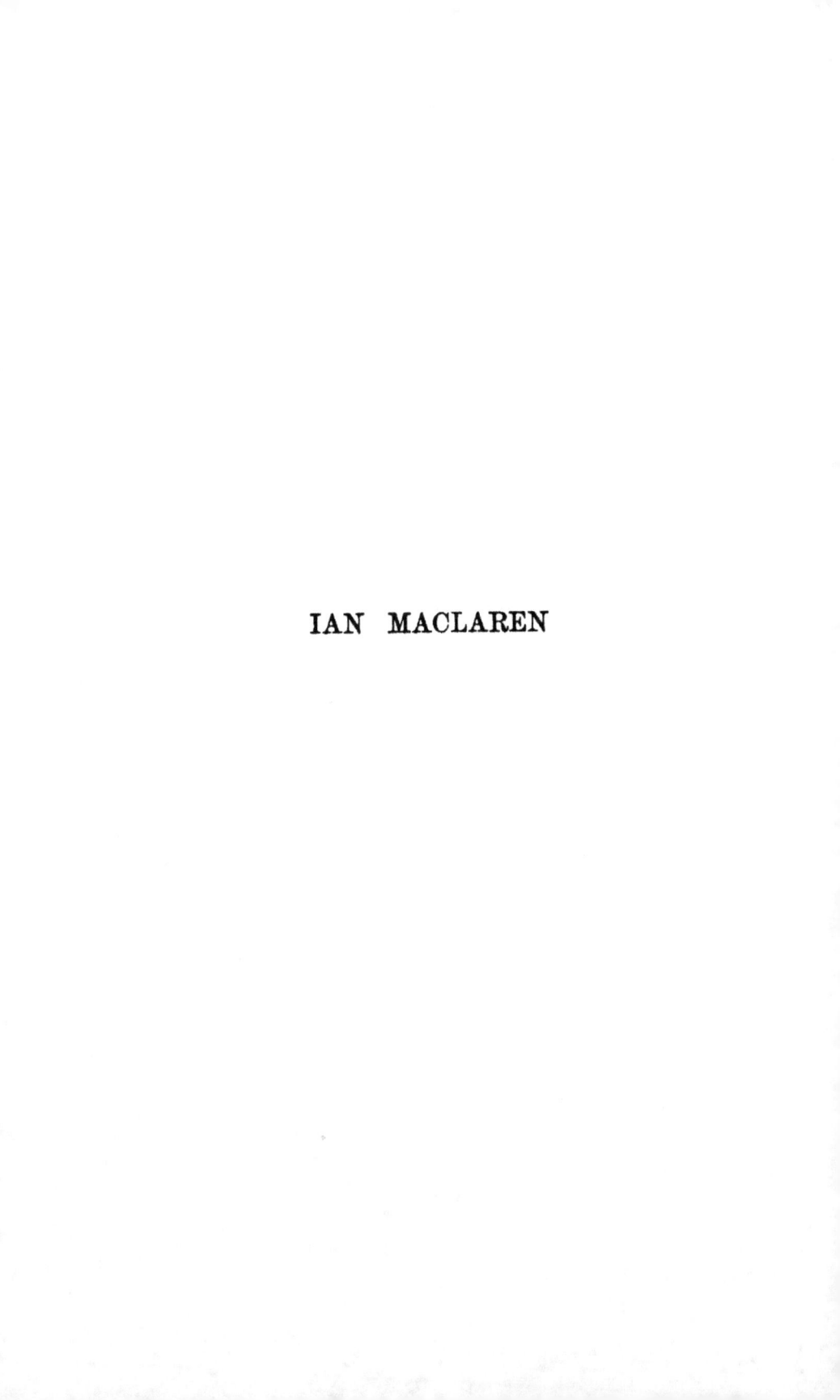

IAN MACLAREN

IAN MACLAREN

So pleased was I with my experience at the Lyceum Theatre that, fearing to off-set the effects upon my nerves of Sir Henry Irving's wonderful cordiality, I made no more visits to the homes of celebrities for two weeks, unless a short call on Li Hung-Chang can be considered such. Mr. Chang was so dispirited over the loss of his yellow jacket and the partition of the Chinese Empire that I could not get a word out of him except that he was not feeling "welly well," and that is hardly sufficient to base an interview on for a practically inexperienced lady journalist like myself.

I therefore returned to English fields

again for my next interview, and having heard that the Rev. Ian Maclaren was engaged on a translation into English of his Scottish stories, I took train to Liverpool, first having wired the famous object of my visit of my intention. He replied instantly by telegraph that he was too busy to receive me, but I started along just the same. There is nothing in the world that so upsets me as having one of my plans go awry, and I certainly do not intend to have my equanimity disturbed for the insufficient reason that somebody else is busy. So I wired back to Liverpool as follows:

"Very sorry, but did not receive your telegram until too late to change my plans. My trunks were all packed and my Scotch lassie costume finished. Expect me on the eleven sixty-seven. Will not stay more than a week.
(Signed)
"ANNE WARRINGTON WITHERUP."

Dr. Maclaren being a courteous man, and I being a lady, I felt confident that this would fetch him; and it apparently did, for two hours later I received this message:

" *Witherup, London:*
"Am not here. Have gone to Edinburgh. Do not know when I shall return.
                (Signed)   "MACLAREN."

To this I immediately replied :

" *Maclaren, Liverpool:*
"All right. Will meet you at Edinburgh, as requested.
                (Signed)   "WITHERUP."

The reader will observe that it takes a smart British author to escape from an American lady journalist once she has set her heart on interviewing him. But I did not go to Edinburgh. I am young, and have not celebrated my thirtieth birthday more than five times, but I am not a gudgeon ; so I refused to be caught by the Edinburgh subterfuge, and stuck to my original proposition of going to Liverpool on the eleven sixty-seven ; and, what is more, I wore my Highland costume, and all the way down studied a Scotch glossary, until I knew the difference between such words as dour and hoots as well as if I had been born and bred at Loch Macglasgie.

As I had expected, Dr. Maclaren was there, anxiously awaiting developments, and as I stepped out of my carriage he jumped from behind a huge trunk by which he thought he was concealed, and fled through the Northwestern Hotel out into the street, and thence off in the direction of the Alexandra Docks. I followed in hot pursuit, and, by the aid of a handy hansom, was not long in overtaking the unwilling author. It may be said by some that I was rather too persistent, and, knowing that the good Doctor did not wish to be interviewed, should have relinquished my quest. It was just that quality in Dr. Maclaren's make-up that made me persist. There are so few successful authors who may be said to possess the virtue of modesty in the presence of

DRESSED FOR THE PART

an interviewer that I determined to catch one who was indeed the only one of that rare class I had ever met.

"Dr. Maclaren?" I cried, as I leaped out of the hansom, and landed, fortunately, on my feet—a lady journalist is a good deal of a feline in certain respects —directly in his path.

"The same," he replied, pantingly. "And you are Miss Witherup?"

"The very same," I retorted, coldly.

"I am perfectly delighted to see you," he said, removing his hat and mopping his brow, which the unwonted exercise he was taking had caused to drip profusely. "Perfectly charmed, Miss Witherup."

I eyed him narrowly. "One wouldn't have thought so," I said, with a suspicious emphasis, "from the way you were running away from me."

"Running away, my dear Miss Witherup?" he gasped, with an admirable affectation of innocence. "Why, not at all."

"Then why, Dr. Maclaren," I asked,

"were you running towards the docks within ten seconds of the arrival of my train?"

To the gentleman's credit be it said that he never hesitated for a moment.

"Why?" he cried, in the manner of one cut to the heart by an unjust suspicion. "Why? Because, madam, when you got out of that railway carriage I did not see you, and fearing that I had mistaken your message, and that instead of coming from London by rail you were coming from America by steamer, I hastened off down towards the docks in the hope of welcoming you to England, and helping you through the custom-house. You wrong me, madam, by thinking otherwise."

The gentleman's tact was so overwhelmingly fine that I forgave him his fiction, which was not quite convincing, and took him by the hand.

"And now," said I, "may I see you at home?"

A gloomy cloud settled over the Doctor's fine features.

112

THE PURSUIT

"That is my embarrassment," he said, with a deep sigh. "I haven't any."

"What?" I cried.

"I have been evicted," he said, sadly.

"You? For non-payment of rent?" I asked, astonished.

"Not at all," said the Doctor, taking a five-pound note from his pocket and throwing it into the street. "I have more money than I know what to do with. For *heresy*. My house belongs to a man who does not like the doctrines of my books, and he put us out last Monday. That is why—"

"I understand," I said, pressing his hand sympathetically. "I am so sorry! But cheer up, Doctor," I added. "I have been sent here by an American newspaper that never does anything by halves. I have been told to interview you at *home*. It must be done. My paper spares no expense. Therefore, when I find you without a home to be interviewed in, I am authorized to provide you with one. Come, let us go and purchase a furnished house somewhere."

He looked at me, astonished.

"Well," he gasped out at length, "I've seen something of American enterprise, but this beats everything."

"I suppose we can get a furnished house for $10,000 ?" I said.

"You can rent all Liverpool for that," he said. "Suppose, instead of going to that expense, we run over to the Golf Links ? I'm very much at home there, though I don't play much of a game."

"Its atmosphere is very Scottish," said I.

"It is indeed," he replied. "Indeed, it's too Scotch for me. I can hold my own with the great bulk of Scotch dialect with ease, but when it comes to golf terms I'm a duffer from Dumfries. There are words like 'foozle' and 'tee-off' and 'schlaff' and 'baffy-iron' and 'Glenlivet.' I've had 'em explained to me many a time and oft, but they go out of one ear just as fast as they go in at the other. That's one reason why I've never written a golf story. The game ought to

114

appeal strongly to me for two reasons—
the self-restraint it imposes upon one's
vocabulary of profane terms, and the
large body of clerical persons who have
found it adapted to their requirements.
But the idiom of it floors me; and after
several ineffectual efforts to master the
mysteries of its glossary, I gave it up. I
can drive like a professional, and my putting is a dream, but I can't converse intelligently about it, and as I have discovered
that half the pleasure of the game lies in
talking of it afterwards, I have given it
up."

By this time we had reached the railway station again, and a great light as of
an inspiration lit up the Doctor's features.

"Splendid idea!" he cried. "Let us
go into the waiting-room of the station,
Miss Witherup. You can interview me
there. I have just remembered that when
I was lecturing in America the greater
part of my time was passed waiting in
railway stations for trains that varied in
lateness between two and eight hours, and

I got to feel quite at home in them. I doubt not that in a few moments I shall feel at home in this one—and then, you know, you need not bother about your train back to London, for it leaves from this very spot in twenty minutes."

He looked at me anxiously, but he need not have. When I discovered that he could not master the art of golfing sufficiently to be able to talk about it at least, he suddenly lost all interest to me. I have known so many persons who were actually only half baked who could talk intelligently about golf, whether they played well or not—the tea-table golfers, we call them at my home near Weehawken—that it seemed to be nothing short of sheer imbecility for a person to confess to an absolute inability to brag about "driving like a professional" and "putting like a dream."

"Very well, Doctor," said I. "This will do me quite as well. I'm tired, and willing to go back, anyhow. Don't bother to wait for my departure."

AT HOME

"Oh, indeed !" he cried, his face suffusing with pleasure. "I shall be delighted to stay. Nothing would so charm me as to see you safely off."

I suppose it was well meant, but I couldn't compliment him on his "putting."

"Are you coming to America again ?" I asked.

"I hope to some day," he replied. "But not to read or to lecture. I am coming to see something of your country. I wish to write some recollections of it, and just now my recollections are confused. I know of course that New York City is the heart of the orange district of Florida, and that Albany is the capital of Saratoga. I am aware that Niagara Falls is at the junction of the Hudson and the Missouri, and that the Great Lakes are in the Adirondacks, and are well stocked with shad, trout, and terrapin, but of your people I know nothing, save that they gather in large audiences and pay large sums for the pleasure of seeing how an author en-

dures reading his own stuff. I know that
you all dine publicly always, and that your
men live at clubs while the ladies are off
bicycling and voting, but what becomes of
the babies I don't know, and I don't wish
to be told. I leave them to the consider-
ation of my friend Caine. When I write
my book, *Scooting through Schoharis; or,
Long Pulls on a Pullman*, I wish it to be
the result of personal observation and not
of hearsay."

"A very good idea," said I. "And
will this be published over your own
name?"

"No, madam," he replied. "That is
where we British authors who write about
America make a mistake. We ruin ourselves if we tell the truth. My book will
ostensibly be the work of 'Sandy Scoot-
mon.'"

"Good name," said I. "And a good
rhyme as well."

"To what?" he asked.

"Hoot mon!" said I, with a certain
dryness of manner.

Just then the train-bell rang, and the London Express was ready.

"Here, Doctor," said I, handing him the usual check as I rose to depart. "Here is a draft on London for $5000. Our thanks to go with it for your courtesy."

He looked annoyed.

"I told you I didn't wish any money," said he, with some asperity. "I have more American fifty-cent dollars now than I can get rid of. They annoy me."

And he tore the check up. We then parted, and the train drew out of the station. Opposite me in the carriage was a young woman who I thought might be interested in knowing with whom I had been talking.

"Do you know who that was?" I asked.

"Very well indeed," she replied.

"Ian Maclaren," I said.

"Not a bit of it," said she. "That's one of our head detectives. We know him well in Liverpool. Dr. Maclaren employs him to stave off American interviewers."

I stared at the woman, aghast.

"I don't believe it," I said. "If he'd been a detective, he wouldn't have torn up my check."

"Quite so," retorted the young woman, and there the conversation stopped.

I wonder if she was right? If I thought she was, I'd devote the rest of my life to seeing Ian Maclaren at home; but I can't help feeling that she was wrong. The man was so entirely courteous, after I finally cornered him, that I don't see how it could have been any one else than the one I sought; for, however much one may object to this popular author's dialect, England has sent us nothing finer in the way of a courteous gentleman than he.

RUDYARD KIPLING

RUDYARD KIPLING

An endeavor to find Rudyard Kipling at home is very much like trying to discover the North Pole. Most people have an idea that there is a North Pole somewhere, but up to the hour of going to press few have managed to locate it definitely. The same is true of Mr. Kipling's home. He has one, no doubt, somewhere, but exactly where that favored spot is, is as yet undetermined. My first effort to find him was at his residence in Vermont, but upon my arrival I learned that he had fled from the Green Mountain State in order to escape from the autograph-hunters who were continually lurking about his estate. Next I sought him at his lodg-

ings in London, but the fog was so thick
that if so be he was within I could not
find him. Then taking a P. & O. steamer,
I went out to Calcutta, and thence to
Simla. In neither place was he to be
found, and I sailed to Egypt, hired a
camel, and upon this ship of the desert
cruised down the easterly coast of Africa
to the Transvaal, where I was informed
that, while he had been there recently,
Mr. Kipling had returned to London. I
immediately turned about, and upon my
faithful and wobbly steed took a short-cut
catacornerwise across to Algiers, where I
was fortunate enough to intercept the
steamer upon which the object of my
quest was sailing back to Britain.

He was travelling *incog.* as Mr. Peters,
but I recognized him in a moment, not
only by his vocabulary, but by his close
resemblance to a wood-cut I had once
seen in the advertisement of a famous
dermatologist, which I had been told was
a better portrait of Kipling than of Dr.
Skinberry himself, whose skill in making

INTERCEPTED THE STEAMER

people look unlike themselves was celebrated by the publication of the wood-cut in question.

He was leaning gracefully over the starboard galley as I walked up the gangplank. I did not speak to him, however, until after the vessel had sailed. I am too old a hand at interviewing modest people to be precipitate, and knew that if I began to talk to Mr. Kipling about my mission before we started, he would in all probability sneak ashore and wait over a steamer to escape me. Once started, he was doomed, unless he should choose to jump overboard. So I waited, and finally, as Gibraltar gradually sank below the horizon, I tackled him.

"Mr. Kipling?" said I, as we met on the lanyard deck.

"Peters," said he, nervously, lighting a jinrikisha.

"All the same," I retorted, taking out my note-book, "I've come to interview you at home. Are you a good sailor?"

"I'm good at whatever I try," said he.

"Therefore you can wager a spring bonnet against a Kohat that I am a good sailor."

"Excuse me for asking," said I. "It was necessary to ascertain. My instructions are to interview you at home. If you are a good sailor, then you are at home on the sea, so we may begin. What work are you engaged on now?"

"The hardest of my life," he replied. "I am now trying to avoid an American lady journalist. I know you are an American by the Cuban flag you are wearing in your button-hole. I know that you are a lady, because you wear a bonnet, which a gentleman would not do if he could. And I know you are a journalist, because you have confessed it. But for goodness' sake, madam, address me as Peters, and I will talk on forever. If it were known on this boat that I am Kipling, I should be compelled to write autographs for the balance of the voyage, and I have come away for a rest."

"Very well, Mr. Peters," said I. "I

ON THE LANYARD DECK

will respect your wishes. Why did you go to South Africa?"

"After color. I am writing a new book, and I needed color. There are more colored people in Africa than anywhere else. Wherefore—"

"I see," said I. "And did you get it?"

"Humph!" he sneered. "Did I get it? It is evident, madam, that you have not closely studied the career of Rudyard —er—Peters. Did he ever fail to get anything he wanted?"

"I don't know," I replied. "That's what I wanted to find out."

"Well, you may draw your own conclusions," he retorted, "when I speak that beautiful and expressive American word 'Nit.'"

I put the word down for future use. It is always well for an American to make use of her own language as far as is possible, and nowhere can one gain a better idea of what is distinctively American than from a study of English authors who use

127

Americanisms with an apology—paid for, no doubt, at space rates.

"Have you been at work on the ocean?" I inquired.

"No," said he. "Why should I work on the ocean? I can't improve the ocean."

"Excuse me," said I. "I didn't know that you were a purist."

"I'm not," said he. "I'm a Peters."

There was a pause, and I began to suspect that beneath his suave exterior Mr. Kipling concealed a certain capacity for being disagreeable.

"I didn't know," I said, "but that you had spent some of your time interviewing the boilers or the engines of the ship. A man who can make a locomotive over into an attractive conversationalist ought to be able to make a donkey-engine, for instance, on shipboard, seem less like a noisy jackass than it is."

"Good!" he cried, his face lighting up. "There's an idea there. Gad! I'll write a poem on the donkey-engine as a sort of companion to my McAndrews Hymn,

128

and, what is more, I will acknowledge my debt to you for suggesting the idea."

"I'm much obliged, Mr.—er—Peters," said I, coldly, "but you needn't. You are welcome to the idea, but I prefer to make my own name for myself. If you put me in one of your books, I should become immortal; and while I wish to become immortal, I prefer to do it without outside assistance."

Peters, né Kipling, immediately melted.

"If you were a man," said he, "I'd slap you on the back and call the steward to ask you what you'd have."

"Thank you," said I. "Under the circumstances, I am glad I am not a man. I do not wish to be slapped on the back, even by a British author. But if you really wish to repay me for my suggestion, drop your unnatural modesty and let me interview you frankly. Tell me what you think — if you ever do think. You've been so meteoric that one naturally credits you with more heart and spontaneity than thought and care."

129

"Very well," said he. "Let the cross-examination begin."

"Do you ride a bicycle?" I asked.

"Not at sea," he replied.

"What is your favorite wheel?" I asked.

"The last that is sent me by the maker," he answered.

"Do you use any tonic—hair, health, or otherwise—which you particularly recommend to authors?" I asked.

"I must refuse to answer that question until I have received the usual check," said Mr.—er—Peters.

"Do you still hold with the Spanish that Americans are pigs, and that New York is a trough?" I asked.

"There are exceptions, and when I last saw New York I was not a conscious witness of any particularly strong devotion to the pen," he answered, uneasily and evasively.

"Do you like the American climate?" I asked.

"Is there such a thing?" he asked, in

return. "If there is, I didn't see it. You Americans are in the experimental stage of existence in weather as in government. I don't think you have as yet settled upon any settled climate. My experience has been that during any week in any season of the year you have a different climate for each day. I can say this, however, that your changes are such that the average is uncomfortable. It is hot one day and cold the next; baking the third; wintry the fourth; humid the fifth; dry the sixth; and on the seventh you begin with sunshine before breakfast, follow it up with rain before luncheon, and a sleigh ride after dinner."

It was evident that Mr. — er — Peters had not lost his powers of observation.

"Why have you left Vermont, Mr. Kipling?" I asked.

"Peters!" he remonstrated, in a beseeching whisper.

"Excuse me, Mr. Peters," said I. "Why have you left Vermont, Mr. Peters?"

"That is a delicate question, madam," he replied. "Are you not aware that my house is still in the market?"

"I am instructed," said I, drawing out my check-book, "to get an answer to any question I may choose to ask, at any cost. If you fear to reply because it may prevent a sale of your house, I will buy the house at your own price."

"Forty thousand dollars," said he. "It's worth twenty thousand, but in the hurry of my departure I left fifty thousand dollars' worth of notes stored away in the attic."

I drew and handed him the check.

"Now that your house is sold," said I, "*why*, Mr. Peters, did you leave Vermont?"

"For several reasons," he replied, putting the check in his pocket, and relighting his jinrikisha, which had gone out. "In the first place, it was some distance from town. I thought, when I built the house, that I could go to New York every morning and come back at night. My

132

notion was correct, but I discovered afterwards that while I could go to New York by day and return by night, there was not more than five minutes between the trains I had to take to do it. Then there was a certain amount of human sympathy involved. The postman was fairly bent under the weight of the letters I received asking for autographs. He came twice a day, and each time the poor chap had to carry a ton of requests for autographs."

"Still, you needn't have replied to them," I said.

"Oh, I never tried to," he said. "It was the postman who aroused my sympathy."

"But you didn't give up trying to live in your own house that had cost you $20,000 for that?" I said.

"Well, no," he answered. "Frankly, I didn't. There were other drawbacks. You Americans are too fond of collecting things. For instance, I went to a reception one night in Boston, and I wore a new dress-suit, and, by Jove! when I got home and took my coat off I found that the tails had been cut off—I presume by souvenir - hunters! Every mail brought countless requests for locks of my hair; and every week, when my laundry came back, there were at least a dozen things of one kind or another missing, which I afterwards learned had been stolen off the line by collectors of literary relics. Then the kodak fiends, that continually lurked about behind bushes and up in the trees and under the piazzas, were a most infernal nuisance. I dare say there are 50,000 unauthorized photographs of myself in existence to - day. Even these I might have endured, not to mention visitors who daily came to my home to tell me how much they had enjoyed my books. Ten or a dozen of these people are gratifying, but when you come down to breakfast and find a line stretching all the way from your front door to the railway station, and excursion trains coming in loaded to the full with others every hour, it ceases to be pleasant and interferes seriously

"HE WAS ERECTING A GRAND-STAND"

with one's work. However, I never mur-
mured until one day I observed a gang of
carpenters at work on the other side of
the street, putting up a curious-looking
structure which resembled nothing I had
ever seen before. When I had made in-
quiries I learned that an enterprising
circus-manager had secured a lease of the
place for the summer, and was erecting a
grand-stand for people who came to catch
a glimpse of me to sit on.

"It was then that the thread of my
patience snapped. I don't mind writing
autographs for eight hours every day; I
don't mind being kodaked if it makes
others happy; and if any Boston relic-
hunter finds comfort in possessing the
tails of my dress-coat he is welcome to
them; but I can't go being turned into a
side-show for the delectation of a circus-
loving people, so I got out."

I was silent. I knew precisely what
he had suffered, and could not blame
him.

"I suppose," I said, sympathetically,

"that this means that you will never return."

"Oh no," said he. "I expect to go back some day, but not until public interest in my personal appearance has died out. Some time somebody will discover some new kind of a freak to interest you people, and when that happens I will venture back for a day or two, but until then I think I will stay over here, where an illustrious personage can have a fit in the street, if he wants to, without attracting any notice whatsoever. There are so many great people over here, like myself and Lord Salisbury and Emperor William, that fame doesn't distinguish a man at all, and it is possible to be happy though illustrious, and to enjoy a certain degree of privacy."

Just then the English coast hove in sight, and Mr. Kipling went below to pack up his mullagatawny, while I drew close to the rail and reflected upon certain peculiarities of my own people.

They certainly do love a circus!

THE DE RESZKES

THE DE RESZKES

ON my return to London I received a message from my principals at home suggesting that, in view of the possibilities of opera next winter, an interview with the famous brothers De Reszke would be interesting to the readers of the United States. I immediately started for Warsaw, where, I was given to understand, these wonderful operatic stars were spending the summer on their justly famous stock-farm.

I arrived late at night, and put up comfortably at a small and inexpensive inn on the outskirts of the city. Mine host was a jolly old Polander, who, having emigrated to and then returned from America, spoke English almost as well as a citizen of the United States. He was very cordial, and assigned me the best room in his house without a murmur or a tip. Anxious to learn how genius is respected in its own country, I inquired of him if he knew where the De Reszkes lived, and what kind of people they were.

"Oh, yais," he said, "I know dem De Reszkes ferry vell already. Dey haf one big farm back on dher hills. I gets my butter undt eggs from dhose De Reszkes."

"Indeed!" said I, somewhat amused. "They are fine fellows, both of them."

"Yais," he said. "I like dem vell enough. Deir butter is goot, undt deir eggs is goot, but deir milk is alvays skimmed. I do not understandt it vy dey shouldt skim deir milk."

"I presume," said I, "that their voices are in good condition?"

"Vell," he replied, "I dondt know much apout deir foices. I dondt effer speak to dem much. Ven I saw dem

140

last dey could make demselves heardt. But, you know, dey dondt needt deir foices much already. Dey keep a man to sell deir butter undt eggs."

"But of course you know that they are renowned for their vocal powers," I suggested.

"I dondt know much apout 'em," he said, simply. "Dey go avay for a year or two every six months, undt dey come back mit plenty ohf money ohf one kind undt anodder, but I subbosed dey made it all oudt ohf butter undt eggs. Vot is dose focal bowers you iss dalking apout? Iss dot some new kindt ohf chiggens?"

I gave the landlord up as a difficult case; but the next day, when I called at the castle of the two famous singers, I perceived why it was that in their own land they were known chiefly as farmers.

"The De Reszkes?" said I, as I entered their castle, some ten miles out of Warsaw, and held out my hands for the brothers to clasp.

It was a superb building, with a façade

of imposing quality, and not, as I had supposed, built of painted canvas, but of granite. To be sure, there were romantic little balconies distributed about it for Jean to practise on, with here and there a dark, forbidding casement which suggested the most base of Édouard's bass notes; but generally the castle suggested anything but the flimsy structure of a grand-opera scene.

Their reply was instant, and I shall never forget the magnificent harmony of their tones as they sang in unison:

"Miss Witherup—Miss Wi-hith-hith-erup?" they inquired.

"The sa-ha-ha-hay-hame!" I sang, and I haven't a bad voice at all.

"We are glad," sang Jean, in tenor tones.

"We are glad," echoed Édouard, only in bass notes, and then they joined together in, "We are glad, we are glad, to see-hee-hee-hee you."

I wish I could write music, so that I could convey the delightful harmonies of

IT WAS A SUPERB BUILDING

the moment to the reader's ear, particularly the last phrase. If a typographical subterfuge may be employed, it went like this:

"To see—

   hee—

      hee—

         hee

           you !"

Start on C, and go a note lower on each line, and you will get some idea of the exquisite musical phrasing of my greeting.

"Excuse me, Jean," said Édouard, "but we are forgetting ourselves. It is only abroad that we are singers. Here we are farmers, and not even yodellists."

"True," said Jean. "Miss Witherup, we must apologize. We recognized in you a matinée girl from New York, and succumbed to the temptation to try to impress you; but here we are not operatic people. We run a farm. Do you come to interview us as singers or farmers?"

143

"I've come to interview you in any old way you please," said I. "I want to see you at home."

"Well, here we are," said Édouard, with one of his most fascinating smiles. "Look at us."

"Tell me," said I, "how did you know I was a matinée girl? You just said you recognized me as one."

"Easy!" laughed Jean, with a wink at his brother. "By the size of your hat."

"Ah, but you said from the United States," I urged. "How did you know that? Don't English matinée girls wear large hats?"

"Yes," returned Édouard, with a courteous bow, "but yours is in exquisite taste."

Just then the telephone-bell rang, and Jean ran to the receiver. Édouard looked a trifle uneasy, and I kept silent.

"What is it, Jean?" Édouard asked in a moment.

"It's a message from the Countess Poniatowska. She says the milk this morning was sour. Those cows must have been at the green apples again," replied the tenor, moodily.

"It's very annoying," put in Édouard, impatiently. "That stage-carpenter we brought over from the Metropolitan isn't worth a cent. I told him to build a coop large enough for those cows to run around in, and strong enough to keep them from breaking out and eating the apples, and this is the third time they've done this. I really think we ought to send him back to New York. He'd make a good target for the gunners to shoot at over at the Navy Yard."

"What are the prospects for grand opera next year, Mr. De Reszke?" I asked, after a slight pause.

"Pretty good," replied Jean, absently. "Of course, if the milk was sour, we'll have to send another can over to the Countess."

"I suppose so," said Édouard; "but the thing's got to stop. I don't mind losing a little money on this farm at the outset, but when it costs us $1500 a quart to raise milk, I don't much like having to provide substitute quarts, when it sours, at sixteen cents a gallon, just because a fool of a carpenter can't build a cow-coop strong enough to keep the beasts away from green apples."

I had to laugh quietly; for, as the daughter of a farmer, I could see that these spoiled children of fortune knew as much about farming as I knew about building light-houses.

"Perhaps," I suggested, "it wasn't the green apples that soured the milk. It may have been the thunder-storm last night that did it."

"That can't be," said Jean, positively. "We have provided against that. All our cows have lightning-rods on them; we bought them from a Connecticut man, who was in here the other day, for $500 apiece, so you see no electrical disturbance could possibly affect them. It must have been the apples."

"I suppose I had better tell Plançon

READY FOR THE STORM

to take the extra quart over himself at once and explain to the Countess," said Édouard.

"Plançon here too?" I cried, in sheer delight.

"Yes; but it's a secret," said Jean. "The whole troupe is here. Plançon has charge of the cows, but nobody knows it. I wouldn't send Plançon," he added, reverting to Édouard's suggestion. "He'll stay over there all day singing duets with the ladies. Why not ask Scalchi to attend to it? She's going to town after the turnip seed this morning, and she can stop on her way."

"All right," said Édouard; "I imagine that will be better. Plançon's got all he can do to get the hay in, anyhow."

Édouard looked at me and laughed.

"We are hard workers here, Miss Witherup," he cried. "And I can tell you what it is, there is no business on earth so exacting and yet so delightful as farming."

"And you are all in it together?" I said.

"Yes. You see, last time we were all

147

in New York we were the most harmonious opera troupe there ever was," Édouard explained, "and it was such a novel situation that Jean and I invited them all here for the farming season, and have put the various branches of the work into the hands of our guests, we two retaining executive control."

"Delightful!" I cried.

"Melba has charge of the dairy, and does a great deal of satisfactory rehearsing while churning the butter. You should hear the Spinning Song from 'Faust' as she does it to the accompaniment of a churn. Magnificent!"

"And you ought to see little Russitano and Cremonini rounding up the chickens every night, while Bauermeister collects the eggs," put in Jean; "and Plançon milking the cows after Maurel has called them home; and that huge old chap Tamagno pushing the lawn-mower up and down the hay-fields through the summer sun—those are sights that even the gods rarely witness."

148

MELBA, THE DAIRY MAID

"It must be a picture!" I ejaculated, with enthusiasm. "And Ancona? Is he with you?"

"He is, and he's as useful a man as ever was," said Édouard. "He is our head ploughboy. And Calvé's vegetable garden—well, Jean and I do not wish to seem vain, Miss Witherup, but really if there is a vegetable garden in the world that produces cabbages that are cabbages, and artichokes that are artichokes, and Bermuda potatoes that are Bermuda potatoes, it is Calvé's garden right here."

"And what becomes of all the product of your farm?" I asked.

"We sell it all," said Jean. "We supply the Czar of Russia with green pease and radishes. The Emperor of Germany buys all his asparagus from us; and we have secured the broiled-chicken contract for the Austrian court for the next five years."

"And you don't feel, Mr. De Reszke," I asked, "that all this interferes with your work?"

"It is my work," replied the great tenor.

"Then why," I queried, "do you not take it up exclusively ? Singing in grand opera must be very exhausting."

"It is," sighed Jean. "It is indeed. Siegfried is harder than haying, and I would rather shear six hundred sheep than sing Tristan ; but, alas, Édouard and I cannot afford to give it up, for if we did, what would become of our farm ? The estimated expense of producing one can of pease on this estate, Miss Witherup, is $300, but we have to let it go at 50 cents. Asparagus costs us $14.80 a spear. A lamb chop from the De Reszke Lambery sells for 60 cents in a Paris restaurant, but it costs us $97 a pound to raise them. So you see why it is that my brother and I still appear periodically in public, and also why it is that our services arc very expensive. We didn't want to take the gross receipts of opera the last time we were in New York, and when the company went to the wall we'd have gladly compromised for 99 cents on the dollar, had we not at that very time received our semi-annual statement from the agent of our farm, showing an expenditure of $800,000, as against gross receipts of $1650."

"Sixteen hundred and thirty dollars," said Édouard, correcting his brother. "We had to deduct $20 from our bill against Queen Victoria for those pheasants' eggs we sent to Windsor. Three crates of them turned out to be Shanghai roosters."

"True," said Jean. "I had forgotten."

I rose, and after presenting the singers with the usual check and my cordial thanks for their hospitality, prepared to take my leave.

"You must have a souvenir of your visit, Miss Witherup," said Jean. "What shall it be—a radish or an Alderney cow? They both cost us about the same."

"Thank you," I said. "I do not eat radishes, and I have no place to keep a cow; but if you will sing the 'Lohengrin'

151

farewell for me, it will rest with me forever."

The brothers laughed.

"You ask too much!" they cried. "That would be like giving you $10,000."

"Oh, very well," said I. "I'll take the will for the deed."

"We'll send you our pictures autographed," said Édouard. "How will that do?"

"I shall be delighted," I replied, as I bowed myself out.

"You can use 'em to illustrate the interview with," Jean called out after me.

And so I left them. I hope their anxiety over their crops will not damage their "focal bowers," as the landlord called them, for with their voices gone I believe their farm would prove a good deal of a burden.

HENRYK SIENKIEWICZ

HENRYK SIENKIEWICZ

On my way back from the Polish home of the De Reszkes it occurred to me that it would be worth while to stop over a day or so and interview Mr. Sienkiewicz. There were a great many things I desired to ask that gentleman, and he is so comparatively unknown a personality that I thought a word or two with him would be interesting.

I had great difficulty in finding him, for the very simple reason that, like most other people, I did not know how to ask for him. Ordinarily I can go into a shop and ask where the person I wish to see may chance to dwell. But when a man has a name like Sienkiewicz, the task is not an easy one. When it is remembered that poets in various parts of the United States have made the name rhyme to such words as sticks, fizz, and even vichy, it will be seen that it requires an unusually bold person to try to speak it in a country where words of that nature are considered as easy to pronounce as Jones or Smith would be in my own beloved land. However, I was not to be daunted, and set about my self-appointed task without hesitation. My first effort was to seek information from my friends the De Reszkes, and I telegraphed them: "Where can I find Sienkiewicz? Please answer." With their usual courtesy the brothers replied promptly: "We don't know what it is. If it is a patent-medicine, apply at any apothecary shop; if it is a vegetable, we do not raise it, but we have a fine line of parsley we can send you if there is any immediate hurry."

I suppose I ought not to give the brothers away by printing their message of reply, but it seems to me to be so interesting that I may hope to be forgiven if I have erred.

I next turned to the book-shops, but even there I was puzzled. Most of the booksellers spoke French; and while I am tolerably familiar with the idiom of the boulevards, I do not speak it fluently, and was utterly at a loss to know what *Quo Vadis* might be in that language. So I asked for a copy of *With Fire and Sword.*

"Avez-vous *Avec Feu et Sabre?*" I asked of the courteous salesman.

It may have been my accent, or it may have been his stupidity. In any event, he did not seem to understand me, so I changed the book, and asked for *The Children of the Soil.*

"N'importe," said I. "Avez-vous *Les Enfants de la Terre?*"

"Excuse me, madame," he replied, in English, "but what do you want, any-how?"

"I want to know where — er — where the author of *Quo Vadis* lives."

"Oh!" said he. "I did not quite understand you. It is so long since I was in Boston that my American French is a trifle weak. If you will take the blue trolley-car that goes up Ujazdowska Avenue, and ask the conductor to let you out at the junction of the Krakowskie Przedmiescie and the Nowy Swiat, the gendarme on the corner will be able to direct you thither."

"Great Heavens!" I cried. "Would you mind writing that down?"

He was a very agreeable young man, and consented. It is from his memorandum that I have copied the names he spoke with such ease, and if it so happens that I have got them wrong, it is his fault, and not mine.

"One more thing before I go," said I, folding up the memorandum and shoving it into the palm of my hand through the opening in my glove. "When I get to —er—the author of *Quo Vadis's* house, whom shall I ask for?"

I fear the young man thought I was
158

mad. He eyed me suspiciously for a moment.

"That all depends upon whom you wish to see," he said.

"I want to see—er—him," said I.

"Then ask for him," he replied. "It is always well, when calling, to ask for the person one wishes to see. If you desired to call upon Mrs. Brown - Jones, for instance, it would be futile to go to her house and ask for Mrs. Pink - Smith, or Mrs. Greene-Robinson."

"I know that," said I. "But what's his name?"

The young man paled visibly. He now felt certain that I was an escaped lunatic.

"I mean, how do you pronounce it?" I hastened to add.

"Oh!" he replied, with a laugh, and visibly relieved. "Oh, that! Why, Sienkiewicz, of course! It is frequently troublesome to those who are not familiar with the Polish language. It is pronounced Sienkiewicz. S-i-e-n-k, Sienk, i-e, ie, w-i-c-z, wicz—Sienkiewicz."

And so I left him, no wiser than before. He did it so fluently and so rapidly that I failed to catch the orthoepic curves involved in this famous name.

Armed with the slip of paper he had so kindly handed me, I sought out and found the trolley-car; conveyed by signs rather than by word of mouth to the conductor where I wished to alight; discovered the gendarme, who turned out to be a born policeman, and was therefore an Irishman, who escorted me without more ado to the house in which dwelt the man for whom I was seeking.

"Is—er—the head of the house in?" I asked of the maid who answered my summons. I spoke in French, and this time met with no difficulty. The maid had served in America, and understood me at once.

"Yes, ma'm," she replied, and immediately ushered me into the author's den, where I discovered the great man himself scolding his secretary.

"I cannot understand why you are so

ASKED A POLICEMAN

careless," he was saying as I entered. "In spite of all my orders, repeatedly given, you will not dot your jays or cross your ells. If you do not take greater care I shall have to get some one else who will. Write this letter over again."

Then he looked up, and perceiving me, rose courteously, and, much to my surprise, observed in charming English :

"Miss Witherup, I presume ?"

"Yes," said I, grasping his proffered hand. "How did you know ?"

"I was at the De Reszkes' when your telegram reached there yesterday," he explained. "We thought you would be amused by the answer we sent you."

"Oh !" said I, seeing that I had been made the victim of a joke. "It wasn't polite, was it ?"

"Oh, I don't know," he replied. "It was inspired by our confidence in your American alertness. We were sure you would be able to find me, anyhow, and we thought we'd indulge in a little humor, that was all."

" Ah !" I said, smiling, to show my forgiveness. " Well, you were right; and now that I have found you, tell me, do you write or dictate your stories ?"

" I dictate them," he said.

" Wonderful !" said I. " Can you really speak all those dreadful Polish words ? They are so long and so full of unexpected consonants in curious juxtaposition that they suggest barb-wire rather than literature to the average American mind."

I had a sort of sneaking idea that he would find in juxtaposition a word to match any of his own, and I spoke it with some pride. He did not seem to notice it, however, and calmly responded :

" One gets used to everything, Miss Witherup. I have known men who could speak Russian so sweetly that you'd never notice how full of jays the language is," said he. " And I have heard Englishmen say that after ten years' residence in the United States they got rather to like the dialect of you New-Yorkers, and in some

THE AUTHOR IN HIS STUDY

cases to speak it with some degree of fluency themselves."

"What is your favorite novel, Mr. — er—"

"Sienkiewicz," he said, smiling over my hesitation.

"Thanks," said I, gratefully. "But never mind that. I have a toothache, anyhow, and if you don't mind I won't—"

"Don't mention it," he said.

"I won't," I answered. "What is your favorite novel?"

"*Quo Vadis*," he replied, promptly, and without any conceit whatever. He was merely candid.

"I don't mean of your own. I mean of other people's," said I.

"Oh!" said he. "I didn't understand; still, my answer must be the same. My favorite novel in Polish is, of course, my own; but of the novels that others have published, I think *Quo Vadis*, by Jeremiah Curtin, is my favorite. Of course it is only a translation, but it is good."

I did not intend to be baffled, however, so I persisted.

"Very well, Mr. — er — You," said I. "What is your favorite novel in Chinese?"

"My favorite novel has not yet been translated into Chinese," he replied, calmly, and I had to admit myself defeated.

"Do you like *Vanity Fair?*" I asked.

"I have never been there," said he, simply.

"What do you think of Pickwick?" I asked.

"That is a large question," he replied, with some uneasiness, I thought. "But as far as my impressions go, I think he was guilty."

I passed the matter over.

"Are you familiar with American literature?" I asked.

"Somewhat," said he. "I have watched the popular books in your country, and have read some of them."

"And what books are they?" I asked.

164

"Well, *Quo Vadis* and *The Prisoner of Zenda*," he replied. "They are both excellent."

"I suppose you never read Conan Doyle," I put in, with some sarcasm. A man who is familiar with what is popular in American literature ought to have read Conan Doyle.

"Yes," he replied, "I have read Conan Doyle. I've read it through three times, but I think Dr. Holmes did better work than that. His *Autograph on the Breakfast Table* was a much better novel than Conan Doyle, and his poem, 'The Charge of the Light Brigade,' is a thing to be remembered. Still, I liked Conan Doyle," he added.

"Everybody does," I said.

"Naturally. It is a novel that suggests life, blood, insight, and all that," said my host. "But of all the books you Americans have written the best is Mr. Thackeray's estimate of your American boulevardier. It was named, if I remember rightly, *Tommie Fadden*. I read that with much interest, and I do not think that Mr. Thackeray ever did anything better, although his story of *Jane Eyre* was very good indeed. Fadden was such a perfect representation of your successful American, and in reading it one can picture to one's self all the peculiar qualities of your best society. Really, I am grateful to Mr. Thackeray for his *Tommie Fadden*, and when you return to New York I hope you will tell him so, with my compliments."

I looked at my watch and observed that the hour was growing late.

"I am returning to Paris," said I, "so I have very little time left. Still, I wish to ask you two questions. First, did you find it hard to make a name for yourself?"

"Very," said he. "It has taken sixteen hours a day for twenty years."

"Then why didn't you choose an easier name, like Lang, or Johnson?" I asked.

"What is your other question?" he said, in response. "When I make a name, I make a name that will be remembered.

166

"ONE MUST BE INTRODUCED"

Sienkiewicz will be remembered, whether it can be pronounced without rehearsal or not. What is your other question?"

"Are you going to read from your own works in America, or not? Dr. Doyle, Dr. Watson, Anthony Hope, Matthew Arnold, and Richard Le Gallienne have done it. How about yourself?" I said.

Mr. Sienkiewicz sighed.

"I wanted to, but I can't," said he. "Nobody will have me."

"Nonsense," said I. "Have you? They'll all have you."

"But," he added, "how can I? One must be introduced, and how can chairmen of the evening introduce me?"

"They have intelligence," said I. And some of them have, so I was quite right.

"Yes, but they have no enunciation or memory," said he. "I can explain forever the pronunciation of my name, but your American chairman can never remember how it is pronounced. I shall *not* go."

And so I departed from the house of Mr. Sienkiewicz.

I can't really see why, when he was making a name for himself, he did not choose one that people outside of his own country could speak occasionally without wrecking their vocal chords — one like Boggs, for instance.

GENERAL WEYLER

GENERAL WEYLER

Upon returning to my London lodgings I was greatly rejoiced to find awaiting me there a cable message from the War Department at Washington, saying that if I would visit General Weyler at Madrid, and secure from him a really frank expression of his views concerning our Spanish imbroglio, the President would be very glad to give me a commission as First Assistant Vivandière to the army of the Philippines, with rank of Captain. I saw at once that in endeavoring to secure an interview with this particular celebrity I ran risks far greater than any I had yet encountered—greater even than those involved in my visit to Mr. Caine at his

Manx home. It is my custom, however, to go wherever duty may call, and inasmuch as my sex has, since the days of Joan of Arc, secured military recognition nowhere except in the ranks of the Salvation Army, I resolved to accept the commission, and notified the War Department accordingly. Fortunately my style of beauty is of the Spanish type, and, furthermore, when at boarding-school, many years ago, in Brooklyn, I had studied the Spanish tongue, so that disguise was not difficult. I had seen Carmencita dance at a private residence in New York, and had therefore some slight knowledge of how a full-fledged señorita should enter a room, so that, on the whole, I went to Madrid tolerably confident that I could beard the great Spanish lion in his den, and escape unscathed.

Purchasing a lace mantilla and a scarlet scarf about eight feet long, my feet covered with red slippers, and a slight suggestion of yellow silk hosiery peeping from beneath a satin skirt of the length

"A RATHER STUNNING BANDERILLO
OPENED THE DOOR"

prescribed by the rainy - day club, and
armed with a pack of cards and a pair of
castanets, I ventured forth upon my per-
ilous mission. Nothing of moment occurred on the journey. I did not don my
Spanish dress until I had left England
behind — indeed, I had reached the Pyr-
enees before I arrayed myself in my costume, although I was most anxious to do
so. It was, after all, so fetching.

Once in Spain I had no difficulty at all,
and in fact made myself very popular with
the natives by telling most charming fort-
unes for them, and dancing the armadil-
lo and opadildock with a verve which
pleased them and surprised even myself.
I have always known myself to be a re-
sourceful creature, but I had never dreamed that among my reserve accomplishments
the agility and grace of a première danseuse
could be numbered.

It was Friday evening when I reached
Madrid, and Saturday morning, bright
and early, I called at General Weyler's
house. A rather stunning banderillo

opened the front door and inquired my business.

"Tell General Weyler," said I, "that Señorita Gypsy del Castillanos de Sierra de Santiago, of Newark, New Jersey, wishes to speak with him on affairs of national importance."

I had resolved upon a bold stroke, and it worked to a charm. The General, who is mortally afraid of assassins, had been listening from his usual hiding-place behind the hat-rack. Pushing the hat-rack from before him, he stepped out into the hall, and, standing between me and the door, inquired threateningly if Newark, New Jersey, was not one of the dependencies of the United States. I answered him in fluent Spanish that it was, told him that I had lived there through no fault of my own for three years, had had to fly before a mob because of my pro-Spanish sympathies, and, travelling night and day, had come to lay before him a complete sketch of the fortifications of Newark, together with the ground-plan of Harlem,

174

IN HIDING.

which, as I informed him, he would have
to take before he could possibly hope to
place Washington in a state of siege. I
also gave him a chart showing by what
waterways a Spanish fleet could approach
and reduce Niagara Falls to ashes — a
blow which would strike England and the
United States with equal force, without
necessarily altering the *status quo ante*
with Great Britain.

The General, like the quick-witted sol-
dier that he is, became interested at once.
The lowering aspect of his brow cleared
like the summer clouds before an August
sun, and, with an urbanity which I had
not expected, invited me to step into his
sanctum. I accepted with alacrity. I
cannot say that it was a pleasant room; it
was in military disorder. Machetes and
murderous-looking pistols were everywhere, and the chair to which I was
assigned was a pleasant little relic of the
Inquisition, and was so arranged that had
the General so wished, the arms holding
hidden iron spikes would fold about me

at any moment and give me a hug I should not forget in a hurry. Added to this was a series of Kodak pictures of all the atrocities of which he was guilty while in Havana. These were framed in one massive oaken frieze running from one end of the room to the other, and labelled on a gilt tablet with black letters, "Snap Shots I Have Snapped, or Pleasant Times in Cuba."

This demonstrates that Weyler is one of those rarely fortunate people who take pleasure and pride in the profession they are called upon to follow.

"General," said I, once we were seated, "did it ever occur to you that if you were two feet shorter, and clean-shaven, with a different nose and a smaller mouth, and a shorter chin and a bigger brow, and less curve to your arms when you walk, you would resemble Napoleon Bonaparte?"

The General was evidently pleased by my compliment.

"Do you think so?" said he, with a smile which absolutely froze my soul.

"I do," I said, meekly, and then I began to weep. I was really unnerved, and began to wish I had never accepted the commission. He was so frightfully cold-blooded, and toyed with a stiletto of razor-like sharpness so carelessly that I was truly terrified.

"Don't cry, Gypsy," he said. "War is a terrible thing, but we will beat those Yankee pigs yet." This, of course, was before peace was declared.

The remark nerved me up again. He believed in me, and that was half the battle.

"Oh, I hope so, General," I sobbed. "But how? Poor old Spain has nothing to fight with."

"Spain has me, señorita!" he cried, passionately. "And I single-handed will give them battle."

"But you do not know the country, General," said I. "Don't risk your life, I beg of you—our only hope! I haven't a doubt that in a fight with pigs you will win; but, General, the United States is so vast, so complicated; it is full of pit-falls!"

I could see that I had him worked up.

"Señorita," he cried, "fear not for Weyler. Think you that I do not know America! Ha-ha! I know its every inch. And let me tell you this: it is because I have devoted hour after hour, day after day, night after night, to the study of the United States, and, best of all, they do not suspect it over there. Why? Because of my strategy! When I wished to learn where was situated the city of Ohio did I send to New York for a map? Not I. I knew that if I bought a map in New York, the house of which I bought it would advertise me as one of their patrons. I am too old a Spaniard to be caught like that." Here his voice sank to a whisper, and, lean-ing forward, he added, impressively: "I sent for a railway time-table. Figures express to my mind what lines or maps could not express to others. What did I learn from the New York Central

178

"I AM TOO OLD A SPANIARD TO BE CAUGHT LIKE THAT"

time - table, for instance ? This : Ohio is twelve hours from New York. Good, say you — but what does that mean ? Travelling at the rate of four miles an hour, Ohio is just forty-eight miles from New York city ! Forty - eight miles ! Pah ! By forced marches our troops could cover that in ten days."

The General snapped his fingers.

"But why Ohio, General ?" I asked.

"The most important city in the American Union," he replied. "Ohio captured, we have the home of McKinley. Ohio captured, we have captured eighty per cent. of the Yankees' public officials. Your Minister of State comes from there ; all the vocal powers of the Senate ; all their political resource. Ah !" he cried, ecstatically, rubbing his hands together, "they little know me ! Let them destroy our navy. Let them take the Philippines. Let them blockade Cuba. Let them do what they please. Spain will wait. Spain will wait a day, a week, a month, a year, a decade, a century—but when least expected, a

179

new fleet, built secretly, a new army, re-
cruiting now on the D. Q." (this is a translation) "will dash into New York Harbor, up the Missouri River, through the
Raritan Canal, and Ohio will lie at our
mercy."

"And then?" said I, overwhelmed.

"We'll hold Ohio until the pig gives
back the Philippines and Cuba," said the
General, suavely.

"Now, General," said I, pursing my lips,
"your plan is a mighty good one, and I
hope you'll try to put it through. But let
me tell you one thing—your time-tables
have misled you. In the first place, any
part of Ohio worth talking of is eighteen
hours from New York by rail, not twelve.
New York Harbor is mined all the way
from Fortress Monroe to the Golden Gate;
and you can't get to Ohio by a dash up
the Missouri River and the Raritan Canal,
because those two waterways above Los
Angeles are not navigable. It is very evident that you, in studying a railroad map,
have forgotten that they are designed to

advertise railroads, and have no geographical significance whatsoever."

"Are you sure?" he asked.

"Perfectly," said I. "I have lived in the country, as I have told you, for three years, and I know what I am talking about."

"Then what shall I do to attack Ohio?" he demanded.

"Well," said I, "the question is not easy to answer, but I think if you would first capture Hoboken—"

"Yes," he said, making a note of my suggestion.

"And then take your transports, guarded by your fighting-ships, out as far as Rahway—" I continued.

"I have it here," said he, putting it down.

"Land your troops there, and send 150,000 south to Bangor, and 100,000 north to Louisville, Kentucky, with a mere handful of sharp-shooters to overawe the Seminoles at Seattle, and then let these troops close in"—said I.

181

"I understand," said he, enthusiastically.

"If you will do that," I put in, "you'll come as near to capturing Ohio as any man can come."

The General rose up and excitedly paced the floor.

"Señorita!" he said, at length, "you have done your country a service. But for you my plans would all have fallen through, because based upon the unreliable information put forth upon an ignorant people by corrupt railway officials. I have studied with care every railway map issued in the United States for ten years past. I had supposed that Ohio could be reached by way of the Missouri and the Raritan. I had supposed that to bring about the fall of Nebraska where their immortal General—for I admit that those pigs have occasionally produced a man—O'Bryan lives, it could be attacked by a land and sea force simultaneously, should the land forces approach the city from the Chicago side, and the fleet pass the forts at Galveston and sail up Chesapeake Bay without further molestation. I see, from what you have told me, that these maps are *falsus in uno* anyhow. I am wondering now if they are not *falsus in omnibus*."

"I shouldn't be surprised if they were even *falsus in trolleybus*," I put in, with a feeble attempt at humor. "Certainly they have misled you, General."

"But," he cried, angrily, "I am not to be thwarted. My ultimate idea remains unchanged. On to Ohio is my watchword. When that falls, the rest will be easy. Thanks to the information you have given, I now know how it may be done, and I assure you, señorita, that you will not be forgotten in the—ah—the—" here his sallow features grew animated, and a flush of real pleasure crossed them as he finished— "in the—ah—reorganization."

"There is to be a reorganization, then?" I asked.

"Yes," he answered. "That is certain,

183

and, on the whole, it is good that there is to be. People are always pleased with that which is novel, and up to this time there have been no kings on the throne bearing the name of Valeriano. *I* think Valeriano the First will make a very pretty autograph. Don't you ?"

"Indeed I do !" I cried. "Write one for me, won't you ?"

But the sagacious warrior merely winked his eye, and by a swish of his machete courteously gave me to understand that the audience was over.

I immediately cabled to Washington the results of my interview, and, by the time I got back to London, had the pleasure of reading in the newspapers that the United States Senate had confirmed my appointment of First Assistant Vivandière to the Department of Manila, with the rank of captain, for services rendered, wherefore I have given up the pleasant task of interviewing celebrities for the sterner duties of war.

I was glad also to learn that the Admin-

184

istration, acting upon my advices, had taken steps to make Ohio impregnable by sea in any event. The Gibraltar of American politics should not be allowed to fall into the hands of a ruthless Castilian like Weyler, and, frankly, whatever else our government will permit, I do not think it will ever do this, and as long as we possess Ohio we need have no fear that we shall be governed by foreign people.

THE END

By CONSTANCE F. WOOLSON

MENTONE, CAIRO, AND CORFU. Illustrated.
Post 8vo, Cloth, Ornamental, $1 75.

DOROTHY, and Other Italian Stories. Illustrated. 16mo, Cloth, Ornamental, $1 25.

THE FRONT YARD, and Other Italian Stories.
Illustrated. 16mo, Cloth, Ornamental, $1 25.

HORACE CHASE. A Novel. 16mo, Cloth,
Ornamental, $1 25.

JUPITER LIGHTS. A Novel. 16mo, Cloth,
Ornamental, $1 25.

EAST ANGELS. A Novel. 16mo, Cloth, Ornamental, $1 25.

ANNE. A Novel. Illustrated. 16mo, Cloth,
Ornamental, $1 25.

FOR THE MAJOR. A Novelette. 16mo, Cloth,
Ornamental, $1 00.

CASTLE NOWHERE. Lake-Country Sketches.
16mo, Cloth, Ornamental, $1 00.

RODMAN THE KEEPER. Southern Sketches.
16mo, Cloth, Ornamental, $1 00.

For swiftly graphic stroke, for delicacy of apprecia-
tive coloring, and for sentimental suggestiveness it
would be hard to rival Miss Woolson's sketches.—
Watchman, Boston.

HARPER & BROTHERS, Publishers
NEW YORK AND LONDON

☞ *Any of the above works will be sent by mail, post-
age prepaid, to any part of the United States, Canada, or
Mexico, on receipt of the price.*

BLACK AND WHITE SERIES

Illustrated. 32mo, Cloth, 50 cents each.

Black and White Series—Continued

THE UNEXPECTED GUESTS. — A LETTER
OF INTRODUCTION. — THE ALBANY DE-
POT. — EVENING DRESS. — A LIKELY
STORY.—THE MOUSE-TRAP.—THE GAR-
ROTERS.—FIVE O'CLOCK TEA. Farces.
Each complete in one volume. By WILLIAM
DEAN HOWELLS.

COFFEE AND REPARTEE. By JOHN KEN-
DRICK BANGS.

THREE WEEKS IN POLITICS. By JOHN
KENDRICK BANGS.

A FAMILY CANOE TRIP. By FLORENCE WAT-
TERS SNEDEKER.

A LITTLE SWISS SOJOURN. By WILLIAM
DEAN HOWELLS.

IN THE VESTIBULE LIMITED. By BRANDER
MATTHEWS.

THIS PICTURE AND THAT. By BRANDER
MATTHEWS.

———

HARPER & BROTHERS, PUBLISHERS

NEW YORK AND LONDON

☞ *Any of the above works will be sent by mail, post-
age prepaid, to any part of the United States, Canada, or
Mexico, on receipt of the price.*

Reprint Publishing

www.ingramcontent.com/pod-product-compliance
Lightning Source LLC
Chambersburg PA
CBHW070325260626
47160CB00003B/956